SPECIAL MESSAGE TO READERS

THE ULVERSCROFT FOUNDATION
(registered UK charity number 264873)
was established in 1972 to provide funds for
research, diagnosis and treatment of eye diseases.
Examples of major projects funded by
the Ulverscroft Foundation are:-

- The Children's Eye Unit at Moorfields Eye Hospital, London
- The Ulverscroft Children's Eye Unit at Great Ormond Street Hospital for Sick Children
- Funding research into eye diseases and treatment at the Department of Ophthalmology, University of Leicester
- The Ulverscroft Vision Research Group, Institute of Child Health
- Twin operating theatres at the Western Ophthalmic Hospital, London
- The Chair of Ophthalmology at the Royal Australian College of Ophthalmologists

You can help further the work of the Foundation
by making a donation or leaving a legacy.
Every contribution is gratefully received. If you
would like to help support the Foundation or
require further information, please contact:

THE ULVERSCROFT FOUNDATION
The Green, Bradgate Road, Anstey
Leicester LE7 7FU, England
Tel: (0116) 236 4325

website: www.foundation.ulverscroft.com

Agatha Christie is known throughout the world as the Queen of Crime. She is the most widely published author of all time and in any language, outsold only by the Bible and Shakespeare. Her first novel, *The Mysterious Affair at Styles*, featuring Hercule Poirot, was written towards the end of the First World War, in which she served as a VAD. She was made a Dame in 1971, and died in 1976.

The only author the Agatha Christie Estate has permitted to produce works in her name, Charles Osborne is a journalist, theatre and opera critic, poet and novelist. He unearthed, translated and adapted Oscar Wilde's previously unproduced play *Constance*, staged at The King's Head Theatre in 2011.

THE UNEXPECTED GUEST

Driving through dense Welsh fog, Michael Starkwedder runs his car into a ditch. After making his way to an isolated house, he discovers Laura Warwick standing near the dead body of her wheelchair-bound husband Richard, revolver in hand. She admits to murder, and her unexpected guest offers to help her concoct a cover story. But it is possible that Laura did not commit the crime after all . . . If so, who is she shielding? The victim's mentally disabled half-brother? Her lover? Perhaps the father of the little boy Richard accidentally killed? The house seems full of possible suspects . . .

Books by Agatha Christie
and Charles Osborne
Published by Ulverscroft:

BLACK COFFEE
SPIDER'S WEB

Agatha Christie

AGATHA CHRISTIE

THE UNEXPECTED GUEST

novelised by Charles Osborne

Complete and Unabridged

ULVERSCROFT
Leicester

First published in Great Britain in 2007 by
Harper
London

First Large Print Edition
published 2015
by arrangement with
HarperCollins*Publishers* Limited
London

A catalogue record for this book is available
from the British Library.

ISBN 978–1–4448–2648–7

Published by
F. A. Thorpe (Publishing)
Anstey, Leicestershire

Set by Words & Graphics Ltd.
Anstey, Leicestershire
Printed and bound in Great Britain by
T. J. International Ltd., Padstow, Cornwall

This book is printed on acid-free paper

Foreword

It was almost certainly because of her dissatisfaction with *Alibi*, someone else's stage adaption in 1928 of her novel, *The Murder of Roger Ackroyd*, that my grandmother Agatha Christie decided to write a play of her own, which is something she had not previously attempted. *Black Coffee*, featuring her favourite detective, Hercule Poirot, was finished by the summer of 1929. But when Agatha showed it to her agent, he advised her not to bother submitting it to any theatre as, in his opinion, it was not good enough to be staged. Fortunately, a friend who was connected with theatrical management persuaded her to ignore such a negative advice, and the play was accepted for production in 1930 at the Embassy Theatre in Swiss Cottage, London.

Black Coffee was favourable received, and in April of the following year transferred to the West End, where it had a successful run of several months at the St Martin's Theatre (where a later Christie play, *The Mousetrap*, began a much longer run in 1952). In 1930, Poirot had been played by a popular actor of the time, Francis L. Sullivan, with John Boxer as his associate Captain Hastings; Joyce Bland played Lucia Amory, and Shakespearian actor Donald Wolfit was Dr Carelli. In the West End production, Francis L. Sullivan was still Poirot, but Hastings was now played by Roland Culver, and Dr Carelli by Dino Galvani.

Some months later, *Black Coffee* was filmed in England at the Twickenham Studios, directed by Leslie Hiscott and starring Austin Trevor, who had already played Poirot in the film version of *Alibi*. The play remained a favourite with repertory companies for some years, and in 1956 Charles Osborne, then earning his living as a young actor, found himself playing Dr Carelli in *Black Coffee* in a summer season at Tunbridge Wells.

Nearly forty years later, after he had in the intervening years not only become a world authority on opera but had also written a splendid book entitled *The Life and Crimes of Agatha Christie*, Osborne remembered the play. He suggested to Agatha Christie Limited (who control the copyright of her works) that, twenty years after the author's death, it would be marvellous to give the world a new Agatha Christie crime novel. We agreed enthusiastically, and the result is this Hercule Poirot murder mystery, which to me reads like authentic, vintage Christie. I feel sure Agatha would be proud to have written it.

Mathew Prichard

1

It was shortly before midnight on a chilly November evening, and swirls of mist obscured parts of the dark, narrow, tree-lined country road in South Wales, not far from the Bristol Channel whence a foghorn sounded its melancholy boom automatically every few moments. Occasionally, the distant barking of a dog could be heard, and the melancholy call of a night-bird. What few houses there were along the road, which was little better than a lane, were about a half-mile apart. On one of its darkest stretches the road turned, passing a handsome, three-storey house standing well back from its spacious garden, and it was at this spot that a car sat, its front wheels caught in the ditch at the side of the road. After two or three attempts to accelerate out of the ditch, the driver of the car must have decided it was no use persevering, and the engine fell silent.

A minute or two passed before the driver emerged from the vehicle, slamming the door behind him. He was a somewhat thick-set, sandy-haired man of about thirty-five, with an outdoor look about him, dressed in a rough tweed suit and dark overcoat and wearing a hat. Using a torch to find his way, he began to walk cautiously across the lawn towards the house, stopping halfway to survey the eighteenth-century building's elegant façade. The house appeared to be in total darkness as he approached the french windows on that side of the edifice which faced him. After turning to look back at the lawn he had crossed, and the road beyond it, he walked right up to the french windows, ran his hands over the glass, and peered in. Unable to discern any movement within, he knocked on the window. There was no response, and after a pause he knocked again much louder. When he realized that his knocking was not having any effect, he tried the handle. Immediately, the window opened and he stumbled into a room that was in darkness.

Inside the room, he paused again, as though attempting to discern any sound or movement. Then, 'Hello,' he called. 'Is anyone there?' Flashing his torch around the room which revealed itself to be a well-furnished study, its walls lined with books, he saw in the centre of the room a handsome middle-aged man sitting in a wheelchair facing the french windows, with a rug over his knees. The man appeared to have fallen asleep in his chair. 'Oh, hello,' said the intruder. 'I didn't mean to startle you. So sorry. It's this confounded fog. I've just run my car off the road into a ditch, and I haven't the faintest idea where I am. Oh, and I've left the window open. I'm so sorry.' Continuing to speak apologetically as he moved, he turned back to the french windows, shut them, and closed the curtains. 'Must have run off the main road somewhere,' he explained. 'I've been driving round these topsy-turvy lanes for an hour or more.'

There was no reply. 'Are you asleep?' the intruder asked, as he faced the man in the wheelchair again. Still receiving no answer, he shone his torch on the face of the chair's occupant, and then stopped abruptly. The man in the chair neither opened his eyes nor moved. As the intruder bent over him, touching his shoulder as though to awaken him, the man's body slumped down into a huddled position in the chair. 'Good God!' the man holding the torch exclaimed. He paused momentarily, as though undecided what to do next, and then, shining his torch about the room, found a light switch by a door, and crossed the room to switch it on.

The light on a desk came on. The intruder put his torch on the desk and, looking intently at the man in the wheelchair, circled

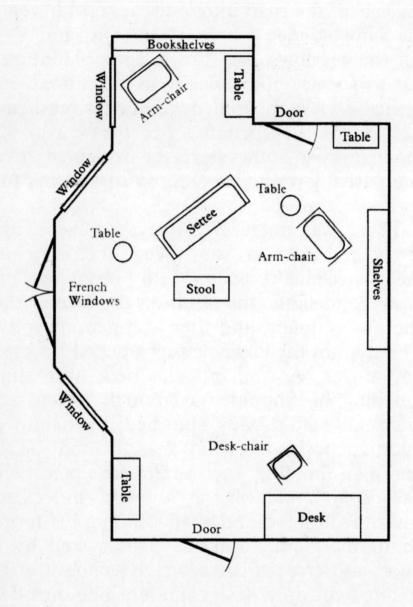

around him. Noticing another door with a light switch by it, he went across and flicked the switch, thus turning on the lamps on two occasional tables strategically placed around the room. Then, taking a step towards the man in the wheelchair, he gave a start as he suddenly noticed for the first time an attractive, fair-haired woman of about thirty, wearing a cocktail dress and matching jacket, standing by a book-lined recess on the opposite side of the room. With her arms hanging limply by her sides, she neither moved nor spoke. It seemed as though she was trying not even to breathe. There was a moment's silence while they stared at each other. Then the man spoke. 'He — he's dead!' he exclaimed.

Completely without expression, the woman answered him.

'Yes.'

'You already knew?' asked the man.

'Yes.'

Cautiously approaching the body in the wheelchair, the man said, 'He's been shot. Through the head. Who — ?'

He paused as the woman slowly brought her right hand up from where it had been hidden by the folds of her dress. In her hand was a revolver. The man drew in his breath sharply. When it seemed that she was not threatening him with it, he approached her, and gently took the gun from her. 'You shot him?' he asked.

'Yes,' the woman replied, after a pause.

The man moved away from her, and put the gun on a table by the wheelchair. For a moment he stood looking at the dead body, and then gazed uncertainly around the room.

'The telephone is over there,' said the woman, nodding towards the desk.

'Telephone?' the man echoed. He sounded startled.

'If you want to ring up the police,' the woman continued, still speaking in the same detached, expressionless manner.

The stranger stared at her as though unable to make her out. Then, 'A few minutes one way or the other won't make any difference,' he said. 'They'll have a bit of a job getting here in this fog anyway. I'd like to know a little more — ' He broke off and looked at the body. 'Who is he?'

'My husband,' replied the woman. She paused, and then continued, 'His name is Richard Warwick. I am Laura Warwick.'

The man continued to stare at her. 'I see,' he murmured finally. 'Hadn't you better — sit down?'

Laura Warwick moved slowly and some-what unsteadily to a sofa. Looking around the room, the man asked, 'Can I get you a — drink — or something? It must have been a shock.'

'Shooting my husband?' Her tone was drily ironic.

Appearing to regain his poise somewhat, the man attempted to match her expression. 'I should imagine so, yes. Or was it just fun and games?'

'It was fun and games,' replied Laura Warwick inscrutably as she sat down on the sofa. The man frowned, looking puzzled. 'But I would like — that drink,' she continued.

The man took off his hat and threw it onto an armchair, then poured brandy from a decanter on the table close to the wheelchair and handed her the glass. She drank and, after a pause, the man said, 'Now, suppose you tell me all about it.'

Laura Warwick looked up at him. 'Hadn't you better ring the police?' she asked.

'All in good time. Nothing wrong with having a cosy little chat first, is there?' He took off his gloves, stuffed them into his overcoat pocket, and started unbuttoning his coat.

Laura Warwick's poise began to break. 'I don't — ' she began. She paused and then continued, 'Who are you? How did you

7

happen to come here tonight?' Without giving him time to answer, she went on, her voice now almost a shout, 'For God's sake, tell me who you are!'

2

'By all means,' the man replied. He ran a hand through his hair, looked around the room for a moment as though wondering where or how to begin, and then continued, 'My name's Michael Starkwedder. I know it's an unusual name.' He spelt it out for her. 'I'm an engineer. I work for Anglo-Iranian, and I'm just back in this country from a term in the Persian Gulf.' He paused, seeming briefly to be remembering the Middle East, or perhaps trying to decide how much detail to go into, then shrugged his shoulders. 'I've been down here in Wales for a couple of days, looking up old landmarks. My mother's family came from this part of the world and I thought I might buy a little house.'

He shook his head, smiling. 'The last two hours — more like three, I should think — I've been hopelessly lost. Driving round all the twisting lanes in South Wales, and ending up in a ditch! Thick fog everywhere. I found a gate, groped my way to this house, hoping to get hold of a telephone or perhaps, if I was lucky, get put up for the night. I tried the handle of the french window there, found it wasn't locked, so I walked in. Whereupon I find — ' He gestured towards the wheelchair, indicating the body slumped in it.

Laura Warwick looked up at him, her eyes expressionless. 'You knocked on the window first — several times,' she murmured.

'Yes, I did. Nobody answered.'

Laura caught her breath. 'No, I didn't answer.' Her voice was now almost a whisper.

Starkwedder looked at her, as though trying to make her out. He took a step towards the body in the wheelchair, then turned back to the woman on the sofa. To encourage her into speaking again, he repeated, 'As I say, I tried the handle, the window wasn't locked, so I came in.'

Laura stared down into her brandy glass. She spoke as though she were quoting. ' "The door opens and the unexpected guest comes in." ' She shivered slightly. 'That saying always frightened me when I was a child. 'The unexpected guest'.' Throwing her head back she stared up at her unexpected visitor, and exclaimed with sudden intensity, 'Oh, why don't you ring up the police and get it over?'

Starkwedder walked over to the body in the chair. 'Not yet,' he said. 'In a moment, perhaps. Can you tell me why you shot him?'

The note of irony returned to Laura's voice as she answered him. 'I can give you some excellent reasons. For one thing, he drank. He drank excessively. For another, he was cruel. Unbearably cruel. I've hated him for years.' Catching the sharp look Starkwedder gave her at this, she continued angrily, 'Oh, what do you expect me to say?'

'You've hated him for years?' Starkwedder murmured as though to himself. He looked thoughtfully at the body. 'But something — something special — happened tonight, didn't it?' he asked.

'You're quite right,' Laura replied emphatically. 'Something special indeed happened tonight. And so — I took the gun off the table from where it was lying beside him, and — and I shot him. It was as simple as that.' She threw an impatient glance at Starkwedder as she continued, 'Oh, what's the good of talking about it? You'll only have to ring up the police in the end. There's no way out.' Her voice dropped as she repeated, 'No way out!'

Starkwedder looked at her from across the room. 'It's not quite as simple as you think,' he observed.

'Why isn't it simple?' asked Laura. Her voice sounded weary.

Approaching her, Starkwedder spoke slowly and deliberately. 'It isn't so easy to do what you're urging me to do,' he said. 'You're a woman. A very attractive woman.'

Laura looked up at him sharply. 'Does that make a difference?' she asked.

Starkwedder's voice sounded almost cheerful as he replied, 'Theoretically, certainly not. But in practical terms, yes.' He took his overcoat over to the recess, put it on the armchair, and returned to stand looking down at the body of Richard Warwick.

'Oh, you're talking about chivalry,' Laura observed listlessly.

'Well, call it curiosity if you prefer,' said Starkwedder. 'I'd like to know what this is all about.'

Laura paused before replying. Then, 'I've told you,' was all she said.

Starkwedder walked slowly around the wheelchair containing the body of Laura's husband, as though fascinated by it. 'You've told me the bare facts, perhaps,' he admitted. 'But nothing *more* than the bare facts.'

'And I've given you my excellent motive,' Laura replied. 'There's nothing more to tell. In any case, why should you believe what I tell you? I could make up any story I liked. You've only got my word for it that Richard was a cruel beast and that he drank and that he made life miserable for me — and that I hated him.'

'I can accept the last statement without

12

question, I think,' said Starkwedder. 'After all, there's a certain amount of evidence to support it.' Approaching the sofa again, he looked down at Laura. 'All the same, it's a bit drastic, don't you think? You say you've hated him for years. Why didn't you leave him? Surely that would have been much simpler.'

Laura's voice was hesitant as she replied, 'I've — I've no money of my own.'

'My dear girl,' said Starkwedder, 'if you could have proved cruelty and habitual drunkenness and all the rest of it, you could have got a divorce — or separation — and then you'd get alimony or whatever it is they call it.' He paused, waiting for an answer.

Finding it difficult to reply, Laura rose and, keeping her back to him, went across to the table to put her glass down.

'Have you got children?' Starkwedder asked her.

'No — no, thank God,' Laura replied.

'Well, then, why didn't you leave him?'

Confused, Laura turned to face her questioner. 'Well — ' she said finally, 'well — you see — now I shall inherit all his money.'

'Oh, no, you won't,' Starkwedder informed her. 'The law won't allow you to profit as the result of a crime.' Taking a step towards Laura, he asked, 'Or did you think that — ?'

He hesitated, and then continued, 'What *did* you think?'

'I don't know what you mean,' Laura told him.

'You're not a stupid woman,' Starkwedder said, looking at her. 'Even if you did inherit his money, it wouldn't be much good to you if you were going to be imprisoned for life.' Settling himself comfortably in the armchair, he added, 'Supposing that I hadn't come knocking at the window just now? What were you going to do?'

'Does it matter?'

'Perhaps not — but I'm interested. What was your story going to be, if I hadn't come barging in and caught you here red-handed? Were you going to say it was an accident? Or suicide?'

'I don't *know*,' Laura exclaimed. She sounded distraught. Crossing to the sofa, she sat facing away from Starkwedder. 'I've no idea,' she added. 'I tell you I — I haven't had time to think.'

'No,' he agreed. 'No, perhaps not — I don't think it was a premeditated affair. I think it was an impulse. In fact, I think it was probably something your husband said. Was that it?'

'It doesn't matter, I tell you,' Laura replied.

'What *did* he say?' Starkwedder insisted. 'What was it?'

14

Laura gazed at him steadily. 'That is something I shall never tell anybody,' she exclaimed.

Starkwedder went over to the sofa and stood behind her. 'You'll be asked it in court,' he informed her.

Her expression was grim as she replied, 'I shan't answer. They can't make me answer.'

'But your counsel will have to know,' said Starkwedder. Leaning over the sofa and looking at her earnestly, he continued, 'It might make all the difference.'

Laura turned to face him. 'Oh, don't you see?' she exclaimed.

'Don't you understand? I've no hope. I'm prepared for the worst.'

'What, just because I came in through that window? If I hadn't — '

'But you did!' Laura interrupted him.

'Yes, I did,' he agreed. 'And consequently you're for it. Is that what you think?'

She made no reply. 'Here,' he said as he handed her a cigarette and took one himself. 'Now, let's go back a little. You've hated your husband for a long time, and tonight he said something that just pushed you over the edge. You snatched up the gun that was lying beside — ' He stopped suddenly, staring at the gun on the table. 'Why was he sitting here with a gun beside him, anyway? It's hardly usual.'

'Oh, that,' said Laura. 'He used to shoot at cats.'

Starkwedder looked at her, surprised. 'Cats?' he asked.

'Oh, I suppose I shall have to do some explaining,' said Laura resignedly.

3

Starkwedder looked at her with a somewhat bemused expression. 'Well?' he prompted.

Laura took a deep breath. Then, staring straight ahead of her, she began to speak. 'Richard used to be a big-game hunter,' she said. 'That was where we first met — in Kenya. He was a different sort of person then. Or perhaps his good qualities showed, and not his bad ones. He did have good qualities, you know. Generosity and courage. Supreme courage. He was a very attractive man to women.'

She looked up suddenly, seeming to be aware of Starkwedder for the first time. Returning her gaze, he lit her cigarette with his lighter, and then his own. 'Go on,' he urged her.

'We married soon after we met,' Laura continued. 'Then, two years later, he had a terrible accident — he was mauled by a lion. He was lucky to escape alive, but he's been a semi-cripple ever since, unable to walk properly.' She leaned back, apparently more relaxed, and Starkwedder moved to a footstool, facing her.

Laura took a puff at her cigarette and then exhaled the smoke. 'They say misfortune improves your character,' she said. 'It didn't improve his. Instead, it developed all his bad points. Vindictiveness, a streak of sadism, drinking too much. He made life pretty impossible for everyone in this house, and we all put up with it because — oh, you know what one says. 'So sad for poor Richard being an invalid.' We shouldn't have put up with it, of course. I see that, now. It simply encouraged him to feel that he was different from other people, and that he could do as he chose without being called to account for it.'

She rose and went across to the table by the armchair to flick ash in the ashtray. 'All his life,' she continued, 'shooting had been the thing Richard liked doing best. So, when we came to live in this house, every night after everyone else had gone to bed, he'd sit here' — she gestured towards the wheelchair — 'and Angell, his — well, valet and general factotum I suppose you'd call him — Angell would bring the brandy and one of Richard's guns, and put them beside him. Then he'd have the french windows wide open, and he'd sit in here looking out, watching for the gleam of a cat's eyes, or a stray rabbit, or a dog for that matter. Of course, there haven't been so many rabbits lately. That disease — what d'you call it? — mixymatosis or whatever — has been killing them off. But he shot quite a lot of cats.' She took a drag on her cigarette. 'He shot them in the daytime, too. And birds.'

'Didn't the neighbours ever complain?' Starkwedder asked her.

'Oh, of couse they did,' Laura replied as she returned to sit on the sofa. 'We've only lived here for a couple of years, you know. Before that, we lived on the east coast, in Norfolk. One or two household pets were victims of Richard's there, and we had a lot of complaints. That's really why we came to live here. It's very isolated, this house. We've only got one neighbour for miles around. But there are plenty of squirrels and birds and stray cats.'

She paused for a moment, and then continued. 'The main trouble in Norfolk was really because a woman came to call at the house one day, collecting subscriptions for the village fête. Richard sent shots to the right and left of her as she was going away, walking down the drive. She bolted like a hare, he said. He roared with laughter when he told us about it. I remember him saying her fat backside was quivering like a jelly. But she went to the police about it, and there was a terrible row.'

19

'I can well imagine that,' was Starkwedder's dry comment.

'But Richard got away with it all right,' Laura told him. 'He had a permit for all his firearms, of course, and he assured the police that he only used them to shoot rabbits. He explained away poor Miss Butterfield by claiming that she was just a nervous old maid who imagined he was shooting at her, which he swore he would never have done. Richard was always plausible. He had no trouble making the police believe him.'

Starkwedder got up from his footstool and went across to Richard Warwick's body. 'Your husband seems to have had a rather perverted sense of humour,' he observed tartly. He looked down at the table beside the wheel-chair. 'I see what you mean,' he continued. 'So a gun by his side was a nightly routine. But surely he couldn't have expected to shoot anything tonight. Not in this fog.'

'Oh, he always had a gun put there,' replied Laura. 'Every night. It was like a child's toy. Sometimes he used to shoot into the wall, making patterns. Over there, if you look.' She indicated the french windows. 'Down there to the left, behind the curtain.'

Starkwedder went across and lifted the curtain on the left-hand side, revealing a pattern of bullet holes in the panelling. 'Good heavens, he's picked out his own initials in the wall. 'R.W', done in bullet holes. Remarkable.' He replaced the curtain, and turned back to Laura. 'I must admit that's damned good shooting. Hm, yes. He must have been pretty frightening to live with.'

'He was,' Laura replied emphatically. With almost hysterical vehemence, she rose from the sofa and approached her uninvited guest. 'Must we go on talking and talking about all this?' she asked in exasperation. 'It's only putting off what's got to happen in the end. Can't you realize that you've *got* to ring up the police? You've no option. Don't you see it would be far kinder to just do it now? Or is it that you want me to do it? Is that it? All right, I will.'

She moved quickly to the phone, but Starkwedder came up to her as she was lifting the receiver, and put his hand over hers. 'We've got to talk first,' he told her.

'We've been talking,' said Laura. 'And anyway, there's nothing to talk about.'

'Yes, there is,' he insisted. 'I'm a fool, I dare say. But we've got to find some way out.'

'Some way out? For me?' asked Laura. She sounded incredulous.

'Yes. For you.' He took a few steps away from her, and then turned back to face her. 'How much courage have you got?' he asked.

21

'Can you lie if necessary — and lie convincingly?'

Laura stared at him. 'You're crazy,' was all she said.

'Probably,' Starkwedder agreed.

She shook her head in perplexity. 'You don't know what you're doing,' she told him.

'I know very well what I'm doing,' he answered. 'I'm making myself an accessory after the fact.'

'But why?' asked Laura. 'Why?'

Starkwedder looked at her for a moment before replying. Then, 'Yes, why?' he repeated. Speaking slowly and deliberately, he said, 'For the simple reason, I suppose, that you're a very attractive woman, and I don't like to think of you being shut up in prison for all the best years of your life. Just as horrible as being hanged by the neck until you are dead, in my view. And the situation looks far from promising for you. Your husband was an invalid and a cripple. Any evidence there might be of provocation would rest entirely on your word, a word which you seem extremely unwilling to give. Therefore it seems highly unlikely that a jury would acquit you.'

Laura looked steadily at him. 'You don't know me,' she said. 'Everything I've told you may have been lies.'

'It may,' Starkwedder agreed cheerfully.

'And perhaps I'm a sucker. But I'm believing you.'

Laura looked away, then sank down on the footstool with her back to him. For a few moments nothing was said. Then, turning to face him, her eyes suddenly alight with hope, she looked at him questioningly, and then nodded almost imperceptibly. 'Yes,' she told him, 'I can lie if I have to.'

'Good,' Starkwedder exclaimed with determination. 'Now, talk and talk fast.' He walked over to the table by the wheelchair, flicking ash in the ashtray. 'In the first place, who exactly is there in this house? Who lives here?'

After a moment's hesitation, Laura began to speak, almost mechanically. 'There's Richard's mother,' she told him. 'And there's Benny — Miss Bennett, but we call her Benny — she's a sort of combined housekeeper and secretary. An ex-hospital nurse. She's been here for ages, and she's devoted to Richard. And then there's Angell. I mentioned him, I think. He's a male nurse-attendant, and — well, valet, I suppose. He looks after Richard generally.'

'Are there servants who live in the house as well?'

'No, there are no live-in servants, only dailies who come in.' She paused. 'Oh — and I almost forgot,' she continued. 'There's Jan, of course.'

'Jan?' Starkwedder asked, sharply. 'Who's Jan?'

Laura gave him an embarrassed look before replying. Then, with an air of reluctance, she said, 'He's Richard's young half-brother. He — he lives with us.'

Starkwedder moved over to the stool where she still sat. 'Come clean, now,' he insisted. 'What is there about Jan that you don't want to tell me?'

After a moment's hesitation, Laura spoke, though she still sounded guarded. 'Jan is a dear,' she said. 'Very affectionate and sweet. But — but he isn't quite like other people. I mean he's — he's what they call retarded.'

'I see,' Starkwedder murmured sympathetically. 'But you're fond of him, aren't you?'

'Yes,' Laura admitted. 'Yes — I'm very fond of him. That's — that's really why I couldn't just go away and leave Richard. Because of Jan. You see, if Richard had had his own way, he would have sent Jan to an institution. A place for the mentally retarded.'

Starkwedder slowly circled the wheelchair, looking down at Richard Warwick's body, and pondering. Then, 'I see,' he murmured. 'Is that the threat he held over you? That, if you left him, he'd send the boy to an institution?'

'Yes,' replied Laura. 'If I — if I believed that I could have earned enough to keep Jan and myself — but I don't know that I could.

24

And anyway, Richard was the boy's legal guardian of course.'

'Was Richard kind to him?' Starkwedder asked.

'Sometimes,' she replied.

'And at other times?'

'He'd — he'd quite frequently talk about sending Jan away,' Laura told him. 'He'd say to Jan, 'They'll be quite kind to you, boy. You'll be well looked after. And Laura, I'm sure, would come and see you once or twice a year.' He'd get Jan all worked up, terrified, begging, pleading, stammering. And then Richard would lean back in his chair and roar with laughter. Throw back his head and laugh, laugh, laugh.'

'I see,' said Starkwedder, watching her carefully. After a pause, he repeated thoughtfully, 'I see.'

Laura rose quickly, and went to the table by the armchair to stub out her cigarette. 'You needn't believe me,' she exclaimed. 'You needn't believe a word I say. For all you know, I might be making it all up.'

'I've told you I'll risk it,' Starkwedder replied. 'Now then,' he continued, 'what's this, what's-her-name, Bennett — Benny — like? Is she sharp? Bright?'

'She's very efficient and capable,' Laura assured him.

Starkwedder snapped his fingers. 'Something's just occurred to me,' he said. 'How is it that nobody in the house heard the shot tonight?'

'Well, Richard's mother is quite old, and she's rather deaf,' Laura replied. 'Benny's room is over on the other side of the house, and Angell's quarters are quite separate, shut off by a baize door. There's young Jan, of course. He sleeps in the room over this. But he goes to bed early, and he sleeps very heavily.'

'That all seems extremely fortunate,' Starkwedder observed.

Laura looked puzzled. 'But what are you suggesting?' she asked him. 'That we could make it look like suicide?'

He turned to look at the body again. 'No,' he said, shaking his head. 'There's no hope of suicide, I'm afraid.' He walked over to the wheelchair and looked down at the corpse of Richard Warwick for a moment, before asking, 'He was right-handed, I assume?'

'Yes,' replied Laura.

'Yes, I was afraid so. In which case he couldn't possibly have shot himself at that angle,' he declared, pointing to Warwick's left temple. 'Besides, there's no mark of scorching.' He considered for a few seconds and then added, 'No, the gun must have been

26

fired from a certain distance away. Suicide is certainly out.' He paused again before continuing. 'But there's accident, of course. After all, it could have been an accident.'

After a longer pause, he began to act out what he had in mind. 'Now, say for instance that I came here this evening. Just as I did, in fact. Blundered in through this window.' He went to the french windows, and mimed the act of stumbling into the room. 'Richard thought I was a burglar, and took a pot shot at me. Well, that's quite likely, from all you've been telling me about his exploits. Well, then, I come up to him' — and Starkwedder hastened to the body in the wheelchair — 'I get the gun away from him — '

Laura interrupted eagerly. 'And it went off in the struggle — yes?'

'Yes,' Starkwedder agreed, but immediately corrected himself. 'No, that won't do. As I say, the police would spot at once that the gun wasn't fired at such close quarters.' He took a few more moments to reconsider, and then continued. 'Well now, say I got the gun right away from him.' He shook his head, and waved his arms in a gesture of frustration. 'No, that's no good. Once I'd done that, why the hell should I shoot him? No, I'm afraid it's tricky.'

He sighed. 'All right,' he decided, 'let's

leave it at murder. Murder pure and simple. But murder by someone from outside. Murder by person or persons unknown.' He crossed to the french windows, held back a curtain, and peered out as though seeking inspiration.

'A real burglar, perhaps?' Laura suggested helpfully.

Starkwedder thought for a moment, and then said, 'Well, I suppose it *could* be a burglar, but it seems a bit bogus.' He paused, then added, 'What about an enemy? That sounds melodramatic perhaps, but from what you've told me about your husband it seems he was the sort who might have had enemies. Am I right?'

'Well, yes,' Laura replied, speaking slowly and uncertainly, 'I suppose Richard had enemies, but — '

'Never mind the buts for the time being,' Starkwedder interrupted her, stubbing out his cigarette at the table by the wheelchair, and moving to stand over her as she sat on the sofa. 'Tell me all you can about Richard's enemies. Number One, I suppose, would be Miss — you know, Miss quivering backside — the woman he took pot shots at. But I don't suppose she's a likely murderer. Anyway, I imagine she still lives in Norfolk, and it would be a bit far-fetched to imagine her taking a cheap day return to Wales to bump him off. Who else?' he urged. 'Who else is there who had a grudge against him?'

Laura looked doubtful. She got up, moved about, and began to unbutton her jacket. 'Well,' she began cautiously, 'there was a gardener, about a year ago. Richard sacked him and wouldn't give him a reference. The man was very abusive about it and made a lot of threats.'

'Who was he?' Starkwedder asked. 'A local chap?'

'Yes,' Laura replied. 'He came from Llanfechan, about four miles away.' She took off her jacket and laid it across an arm of the sofa.

Starkwedder frowned. 'I don't think much of your gardener,' he told her. 'You can bet he's got a nice, stay-at-home alibi. And if he hasn't got an alibi, or it's an alibi that only his wife can confirm or support, we might end up getting the poor chap convicted for some-thing he hasn't done. No, that's no good. What we want is some enemy out of the past, who wouldn't be so easy to track down.'

Laura moved slowly around the room, trying to think, as Starkwedder continued, 'How about someone from Richard's tiger- and lion-shooting days? Someone in Kenya, or South Africa, or India? Some place where the police can't check up on him very easily.'

'If I could only think,' said Laura, despairingly. 'If I could only remember. If I could remember some of the stories about those days that Richard told us at one time or another.'

'It isn't even as though we'd got any nice props handy,' Starkwedder muttered. 'You know, a Sikh turban carelessly draped over the decanter, or a Mau Mau knife, or a poisoned arrow.' He pressed his hands to his forehead in concentration. 'Damn it all,' he went on, 'what we want is someone with a grudge, someone who'd been kicked around by Richard.' Approaching Laura, he urged her, 'Think, woman. Think. Think!'

'I — I *can't* think,' replied Laura, her voice almost breaking with frustration.

'You've told me the kind of man your husband was. There must have been incidents, people. Heavens above, there must have been *something*,' he exclaimed.

Laura paced about the room, trying desperately to remember.

'Someone who made threats. Justifiable threats, perhaps,' Starkwedder encouraged her.

Laura stopped her pacing, and turned to face him. 'There was — I've just remembered,' she said. She spoke slowly. 'There was a man whose child Richard ran over.'

4

Starkwedder stared at Laura. 'Richard ran over a child?' he asked excitedly. 'When was this?'

'It was about two years ago,' Laura told him. 'When we were living in Norfolk. The child's father certainly made threats at the time.'

Starkwedder sat down on the footstool. 'Now, that sounds like a possibility,' he said. 'Anyway, tell me all you can remember about him.'

Laura thought for a moment, and then began to speak. 'Richard was driving back from Cromer,' she said. 'He'd had far too much to drink, which was by no means unusual. He drove through a little village at about sixty miles an hour, apparently zig-zagging quite a bit. The child — a little boy — ran out into the road from the inn there — Richard knocked him down and he was killed instantly.'

'Do you mean,' Starkwedder asked her, 'that your husband could drive a car, despite his disability?'

'Yes, he could. Oh, it had to be specially

built, with special controls that he could manage, but, yes, he was able to drive that vehicle.'

'I see,' said Starkwedder. 'What happened about the child? Surely the police could have got Richard for manslaughter?'

'There was an inquest, of course,' Laura explained. A bitter note crept into her voice as she added, 'Richard was exonerated completely.'

'Were there any witnesses?' Starkwedder asked her.

'Well,' Laura replied, 'there was the child's father. He saw it happen. But there was also a hospital nurse — Nurse Warburton — who was in the car with Richard. She gave evidence, of course. And according to her, the car was going under thirty miles an hour and Richard had had only one glass of sherry. She said that the accident was quite unavoidable — the little boy just suddenly rushed out, straight in front of the car. They believed *her*, and not the child's father who said that the car was being driven erratically and at a very high speed. I understand the poor man was — rather over-violent in expressing his feelings.' Laura moved to the armchair, adding, 'You see, anyone *would* believe Nurse Warburton. She seemed the very essence of honesty and reliability and accuracy and careful understatement and all that.'

'You weren't in the car yourself?' Starkwedder asked.

'No, I wasn't,' Laura replied. 'I was at home.'

'Then how do you know that what Nurse what's-her-name said mightn't have been the truth?'

'Oh, the whole thing was very freely discussed by Richard,' she said bitterly. 'After they came back from the inquest, I remember very clearly. He said, 'Bravo, Warby, jolly good show. You've probably got me off quite a stiff jail sentence.' And she said, 'You don't deserve to have got off, Mr Warwick. You know you were driving much too fast. It's a shame about that poor child.' And then Richard said, 'Oh, forget it! I've made it worth your while. Anyway, what's one brat more or less in this overcrowded world? He's just as well out of it all. It's not going to spoil my sleep, I assure you.''

Starkwedder rose from the stool and, glancing over his shoulder at Richard Warwick's body, said grimly, 'The more I hear about your husband, the more I'm willing to believe that what happened tonight was justifiable homicide rather than murder.' Approaching Laura, he continued, 'Now then. This man whose child was run over. The boy's father. What's his name?'

'A Scottish name, I think,' Laura replied. 'Mac — Mac something — MacLeod? MacCrae? — I can't remember.'

'But you've got to try to remember,' Starkwedder insisted. 'Come on, you must. Is he still living in Norfolk?'

'No, no,' said Laura. 'He was only over here for a visit. To his wife's relations, I think. I seem to remember he came from Canada.'

'Canada — that's a nice long way away,' Starkwedder observed. 'It would take time to chase up. Yes,' he continued, moving to behind the sofa, 'yes, I think there are possibilities there. But for God's sake try to remember the man's name.' He went across to his overcoat on the armchair in the recess, took his gloves from a pocket, and put them on. Then, looking searchingly around the room, he asked, 'Got any newspapers about?'

'Newspapers?' Laura asked, surprised.

'Not today's,' he explained. 'Yesterday's or the day before would do better.'

Rising from the sofa, Laura went to a cupboard behind the armchair. 'There are some old ones in the cupboard here. We keep them for lighting fires,' she told him.

Starkwedder joined her, opened the cupboard door, and took out a newspaper. After checking the date, he announced, 'This is

34

fine. Just what we want.' He closed the cupboard door, took the newspaper to the desk, and from a pigeon-hole on the desk extracted a pair of scissors.

'What are you going to do?' asked Laura.

'We're going to manufacture some evidence.' He clicked the scissors as though to demonstrate.

Laura stared at him, perplexed. 'But suppose the police succeed in finding this man,' she asked. 'What happens then?'

Starkwedder beamed at her. 'If he still lives in Canada, it'll take a bit of doing,' he announced with an air of smugness. 'And by the time they do find him, he'll no doubt have an alibi for tonight. Being a few thousand miles away ought to be satisfactory enough. And by then it will be a bit late for them to check up on things here. Anyway, it's the best we can do. It'll give us breathing space at all events.'

Laura looked worried. 'I don't like it,' she complained.

Starkwedder gave her a somewhat exasperated look. 'My dear girl,' he admonished her, 'you can't afford to be choosy. But you must try to remember that man's name.'

'I can't, I tell you, I can't,' Laura insisted.

'Was it MacDougall, perhaps? Or Mackintosh?' he suggested helpfully.

Laura took a few steps away from him, putting her hands to her ears. 'Do stop,' she cried. 'You're only making it worse. I'm not sure now that it was Mac anything.'

'Well, if you can't remember, you can't,' Starkwedder conceded. 'We shall have to manage without. You don't remember the date, by any chance, or anything useful like that?'

'Oh, I can tell you the date, all right,' said Laura. 'It was May the fifteenth.'

Surprised, Starkwedder asked, 'Now, how on earth can you remember that?'

There was bitterness in Laura's voice as she replied, 'Because it happened on my birthday.'

'Ah, I see — yes — well, that solves one little problem,' observed Starkwedder. 'And we've also got one little piece of luck. This paper is dated the fifteenth.' He cut the date out carefully from the newspaper.

Joining him at the desk and looking over his shoulder, Laura pointed out that the date on the newspaper was November the fifteenth, not May. 'Yes,' he admitted, 'but it's the numbers that are the more awkward. Now, May. May's a short word — ah, yes, here's an M. Now an A, and a Y.'

'What in heaven's name are you doing?' Laura asked.

Starkwedder's only response, as he seated himself in the desk chair, was, 'Got any paste?'

Laura was about to take a pot of paste from a pigeon-hole, but he stopped her. 'No, don't touch,' he instructed. 'We don't want your fingerprints on it.' He took the pot of paste in his gloved hands, and removed the lid. 'How to be a criminal in one easy lesson,' he continued. 'And, yes, here's a plain block of writing paper — the kind sold all over the British Isles.' Taking a notepad from the pigeon-hole, he proceeded to paste words and letters onto a sheet of notepaper. 'Now, watch this, one — two — three — a bit tricky with gloves. But there we are. 'May fifteen. Paid in full.' Oh, the 'in' has come off.' He pasted it back on again. 'There, now. How do you like that?'

He tore the sheet off the pad and showed it to her, then went across to Richard Warwick's body in its wheelchair. 'We'll tuck it neatly into his jacket pocket, like that.' As he did so, he dislodged a pocket lighter, which fell to the floor. 'Hello, what's this?'

Laura gave a sharp exclamation and tried to snatch the lighter up, but Starkwedder had already done so, and was examining it. 'Give it to me,' cried Laura breathlessly. 'Give it to me!'

Looking faintly surprised, Starkwedder handed it to her. 'It's — it's my lighter,' she explained, unnecessarily.

'All right, so it's your lighter,' he agreed. 'That's nothing to get upset about.' He looked at her curiously. 'You're not losing your nerve, are you?'

She walked away from him to the sofa. As she did so, she rubbed the lighter on her skirt as though to remove possible fingerprints, taking care to ensure that Starkwedder did not observe her doing so. 'No, of course I'm not losing my nerve,' she assured him.

Having made certain that the pasted-up message from the newspaper in Richard Warwick's breast pocket was tucked securely under the lapel, Starkwedder went over to the desk, replaced the lid of the paste-pot, removed his gloves, took out a handkerchief, and looked at Laura. 'There we are!' he announced. 'All ready for the next step. Where's that glass you were drinking out of just now?'

Laura retrieved the glass from the table where she had deposited it. Leaving her lighter on the table, she returned with the glass to Starkwedder. He took it from her, and was about to wipe off her fingerprints, but then stopped. 'No,' he murmured. 'No, that would be stupid.'

'Why?' asked Laura.

'Well, there ought to be fingerprints,' he explained, 'both on the glass and on the decanter. This valet fellow's, for one, and probably your husband's as well. No fingerprints at all would look very fishy to the police.' He took a sip from the glass he was holding. 'Now I must think of a way to explain mine,' he added. 'Crime isn't easy, is it?'

With sudden passion, Laura exclaimed, 'Oh, don't! Don't get mixed up in this. They might suspect *you*.'

Amused, Starkwedder replied, 'Oh, I'm a very respectable chap — quite above suspicion. But, in a sense I *am* mixed up in it already. After all, my car's out there, stuck fast in the ditch. But don't worry, just a spot of perjury and a little tinkering with the time element — that's the worst they'd be able to bring against me. And they won't, if you play your part properly.'

Frightened, Laura sat on the footstool, with her back to him. He came round to face her. 'Now then,' he said, 'are you ready?'

'Ready — for what?' asked Laura.

'Come on, you must pull yourself together,' he urged her.

Sounding dazed, she murmured, 'I feel — stupid — I — I can't think.'

'You don't have to think,' Starkwedder told

her. 'You've just got to obey orders. Now then, here's the blueprint. First, have you got a furnace of any kind in the house?'

'A furnace?' Laura thought, and then replied, 'Well, there's the water boiler.'

'Good.' He went to the desk, took the newspaper, and rolled up the scraps of paper in it. Returning to Laura, he handed her the bundle. 'Now then,' he instructed her, 'the first thing you do is to go into the kitchen and put this in the boiler. Then you go upstairs, get out of your clothes and into a dressing-gown — or negligée, or what-have-you.' He paused. 'Have you got any aspirin?'

Puzzled, Laura replied, 'Yes.'

As though thinking and planning as he spoke, Starkwedder continued, 'Well — empty the bottle down the loo. Then go along to some-one — your mother-in-law, or Miss — what is it — Bennett? — and say you've got a head-ache and want some aspirin. Then, while you're with whoever it is — leave the door open, by the way — you'll hear the shot.'

'What shot?' asked Laura, staring at him.

Without replying, Starkwedder crossed to the table by the wheelchair and picked up the gun. 'Yes, yes,' he murmured absently, 'I'll attend to that.' He examined the gun. 'Hm. Looks foreign to me — war souvenir, is it?'

Laura rose from the stool. 'I don't know,'

she told him. 'Richard had several foreign makes of pistol.'

'I wonder if it's registered,' Starkwedder said, almost to himself, still holding the gun.

Laura sat on the sofa. 'Richard had a licence — if that's what you call it — a permit for his collection,' she said.

'Yes, I suppose he would have. But that doesn't mean that they would all be registered in his name. In practice, people are often rather careless about that kind of thing. Is there anyone who'd be likely to know definitely?'

'Angell might,' said Laura. 'Does it matter?'

Starkwedder moved about the room as he replied. 'Well, the way we're building this up, old MacThing — the father of the child Richard ran over — is more likely to come bursting in, breathing blood and thunder and revenge, with his own weapon at the ready. But one could, after all, make out quite a plausible case the other way. This man — whoever he is — bursts in. Richard, only half awake, snatches up his gun. The other fellow wrenches it away from him, and shoots. I admit it sounds a bit far-fetched, but it'll have to do. We've got to take some risks, it just can't be avoided.'

He placed the gun on the table by the wheelchair, and approached her. 'Now then,' he continued, 'have we thought of everything? I hope so. The fact that he was shot a quarter of an hour or twenty minutes earlier won't be apparent by the time the police get here. Driving along these roads in this fog won't be easy for them.' He went over to the curtain by the french windows, lifted it, and looked at the bullet holes in the wall. ''R.W'. Very nice. I'll try to add a full stop.'

Replacing the curtain, he came back to her. 'When you hear the shot,' he instructed Laura, 'what you do is register alarm, and bring Miss Bennett — or anyone else you can collect — down here. Your story is that you don't know anything. You went to bed, you woke up with a violent headache, you went along to look for aspirin — and that's *all* you know. Understand?'

Laura nodded.

'Good,' said Starkwedder. 'All the rest you leave to me. Are you feeling all right now?'

'Yes, I think so,' Laura whispered.

'Then go along and do your stuff,' he ordered her.

Laura hesitated. 'You — you oughtn't to do this,' she urged him again. 'You oughtn't. You shouldn't get involved.'

'Now, don't let's have any more of that,' Starkwedder insisted. 'Everyone has their own form of — what did we call it just now?

42

— fun and games. You had your fun and games shooting your husband. I'm having my fun and games now. Let's just say I've always had a secret longing to see how I could get on with a detective story in real life.' He gave her a quick, reassuring smile. 'Now, can you do what I've told you?'

Laura nodded. 'Yes.'

'Right. Oh, I see you've got a watch. Good. What time do you make it?'

Laura showed him her wristwatch, and he set his accordingly. 'Just after ten minutes to,' he observed. 'I'll allow you three — no, four — minutes. Four minutes to go along to the kitchen, pop that paper in the boiler, go upstairs, get out of your things and into a dressing-gown, and along to Miss Bennett or whoever. Do you think you can do that, Laura?' He smiled at her reassuringly.

Laura nodded.

'Now then,' he continued, 'at five minutes to midnight exactly, you'll hear the shot. Off you go.'

Moving to the door, she turned and looked at him, uncertain of herself. Starkwedder went across to open the door for her. 'You're not going to let me down, are you?' he asked.

'No,' replied Laura faintly.

'Good.'

Laura was about to leave the room when

Starkwedder noticed her jacket lying on the arm of the sofa. Calling her back, he gave it to her, smiling. She went out, and he closed the door behind her.

5

After closing the door behind Laura, Starkwedder paused, working out in his mind what was to be done. After a moment, he glanced at his watch, then took out a cigarette. He moved to the table by the armchair and was about to pick up the lighter when he noticed a photograph of Laura on one of the bookshelves. He picked it up, looked at it, smiled, replaced it, and lit a cigarette, leaving the lighter on the table. Taking out his handkerchief, he rubbed any fingerprints off the arms of the armchair and the photograph, and then pushed the chair back to its original position. He took Laura's cigarette from the ashtray, then went to the table by the wheelchair and took his own stub from the ashtray. Crossing to the desk, he next rubbed any fingerprints from it, replaced the scissors and notepad, and adjusted the blotter. He looked around him on the floor for any scrap of paper that might have been missed, found one near the desk, screwed it up and put it in his trousers pocket. He rubbed fingerprints off the light switch by the door and off the desk chair, picked up his

45

torch from the desk, went over to the french windows, drew the curtain back slightly, and shone the torch through the window onto the path outside.

'Too hard for footprints,' he murmured to himself. He put the torch on the table by the wheelchair and picked up the gun. Making sure that it was sufficiently loaded, he polished it for fingerprints, then went to the stool and put the gun down on it. After glancing again at his watch, he went to the armchair in the recess and put on his hat, scarf and gloves. With his overcoat on his arm, he crossed to the door. He was about to switch off the lights when he remembered to remove the fingerprints from the door-plate and handle. He then switched off the lights, and came back to the stool, putting his coat on. He picked up the gun, and was about to fire it at the initials on the wall when he realized that they were hidden by the curtain.

'Damn!' he muttered. Quickly taking the desk chair, he used it to hold the curtain back. He returned to his position by the stool, fired the gun, and then quickly went back to the wall to examine the result. 'Not bad!' he congratulated himself.

As he replaced the desk chair in its proper position, Starkwedder could hear voices in the hall. He rushed off through the french windows, taking the gun with him. A moment later he reappeared, snatched up the torch, and dashed out again.

From various parts of the house, four people hurried towards the study. Richard Warwick's mother, a tall, commanding old lady, was in her dressing-gown. She looked pallid and walked with the aid of a stick. 'What is it, Jan?' she asked the teenage boy in pyjamas with the strange, rather innocent, faun-like face, who was close behind her on the landing. 'Why is everybody wandering about in the middle of the night?' she exclaimed as they were joined by a grey-haired, middle-aged woman, wearing a sensible flannel dressing-gown. 'Benny,' she ordered the woman, 'tell me what's going on.'

Laura was close behind, and Mrs Warwick continued, 'Have you all taken leave of your senses? Laura, what's happened? Jan — Jan — will someone tell me what is going on in this house?'

'I'll bet it's Richard,' said the boy, who looked about nineteen, though his voice and manner were those of a younger child. 'He's shooting at the fog again.' There was a note of petulance in his voice as he added, 'Tell him he's not to shoot and wake us all up out of our beauty sleep. I was deep asleep, and so was Benny. Weren't you, Benny? Be careful,

Laura, Richard's dangerous. He's dangerous, Benny, be careful.'

'There's thick fog outside,' said Laura, looking through the landing window. 'You can barely make out the path. I can't imagine what he can be shooting at in this mist. It's absurd. Besides, I thought I heard a cry.'

Miss Bennett — Benny — an alert, brisk woman who looked like the ex-hospital nurse that she was, spoke somewhat officiously. 'I really can't see why you're so upset, Laura. It's just Richard amusing himself as usual. But I didn't hear any shooting. I'm sure there's nothing wrong. I think you're imagining things. But he's certainly very selfish and I shall tell him so. Richard,' she called as she entered the study, 'really, Richard, it's too bad at this time of night. You frightened us — Richard!'

Laura, wearing her dressing-gown, followed Miss Bennett into the room. As she switched on the lights and moved to the sofa, the boy Jan followed her. He looked at Miss Bennett who stood staring at Richard Warwick in his wheelchair. 'What is it, Benny?' asked Jan. 'What's the matter?'

'It's Richard,' said Miss Bennett, her voice strangely calm. 'He's killed himself.'

'Look,' cried young Jan excitedly, pointing at the table. 'Richard's revolver's gone.'

A voice from outside in the garden called,

48

'What's going on in there? Is anything wrong?' Looking through the small window in the recess, Jan shouted, 'Listen! There's someone outside!'

'Outside?' said Miss Bennett. 'Who?' She turned to the french windows and was about to draw back the curtain when Starkwedder suddenly appeared. Miss Bennett stepped back in alarm as Starkwedder came forward, asking urgently, 'What's happened here? What's the matter?' His glance fell on Richard Warwick in the wheelchair. 'This man's dead!' he exclaimed. 'Shot.' He looked around the room suspiciously, taking them all in.

'Who are you?' asked Miss Bennett. 'Where did you come from?'

'Just run my car into a ditch,' replied Starkwedder. 'I've been lost for hours. Found some gates and came up to the house to try to get some help and telephone. Heard a shot, and someone came rushing out of the windows and collided with me.' Holding out the gun, Starkwedder added, 'He dropped this.'

'Where did this man go?' Miss Bennett asked him.

'How the hell should I know in this fog?' Starkwedder replied.

Jan stood in front of Richard's body, staring excitedly at it. 'Somebody's shot

49

Richard,' he shouted.

'Looks like it,' Starkwedder agreed. 'You'd better get in touch with the police.' He placed the gun on the table by the wheelchair, picked up the decanter, and poured brandy into a glass. 'Who is he?'

'My husband,' said Laura, expressionlessly, as she went to sit on the sofa.

With what sounded a slightly forced concern, Starkwedder said to her, 'Here — drink this.' Laura looked up at him. 'You've had a shock,' he added emphatically. As she took the glass, with his back turned to the others Starkwedder gave her a conspiratorial grin, to call her attention to his solution of the fingerprint problem. Turning away, he threw his hat on the armchair, and then, suddenly noticing that Miss Bennett was about to bend over Richard Warwick's body, he swung quickly round. 'No, don't touch anything, madam,' he implored her. 'This looks like murder, and if it is then nothing must be touched.'

Straightening up, Miss Bennett backed away from the body in the chair, looking appalled. 'Murder?' she exclaimed. 'It can't be murder!'

Mrs Warwick, the mother of the dead man, had stopped just inside the door of the study. She came forward now, asking, 'What has happened?'

'Richard's been shot! Richard's been shot!' Jan told her. He sounded more excited than concerned.

'Quiet, Jan,' ordered Miss Bennett.

'What did I hear you say?' asked Mrs Warwick, quietly.

'*He* said — murder,' Benny told her, indicating Starkwedder.

'Richard,' Mrs Warwick whispered, as Jan leaned over the body, calling, 'Look — look — there's something on his chest — a paper — with writing on it.' His hand went out to it, but he was stopped by Starkwedder's command: 'Don't touch — whatever you do, don't touch.' Then he read aloud, slowly, ' "May — fifteen — paid in full".'

'Good Lord! MacGregor,' Miss Bennett exclaimed, moving behind the sofa.

Laura rose. Mrs Warwick frowned. 'You mean,' she said, ' — that man — the father — the child that was run over — ?'

'Of course, MacGregor,' Laura murmured to herself as she sat in the armchair.

Jan went up to the body. 'Look — it's all newspaper — cut up,' he said in excitement. Starkwedder again restrained him. 'No, don't touch it,' he ordered. 'It's got to be left for the police.' He stepped towards the telephone. 'Shall I — ?'

'No,' said Mrs Warwick firmly. 'I will.'

Taking charge of the situation, and summoning her courage, she went to the desk and started to dial. Jan moved excitedly to the stool and knelt upon it. 'The man that ran away,' he asked Miss Bennett. 'Do you think he — ?'

'Ssh, Jan,' Miss Bennett said to him firmly, while Mrs Warwick spoke quietly but in a clear, authoritative voice on the telephone. 'Is that the police station? This is Llangelert House. Mr Richard Warwick's house. Mr Warwick has just been found — shot dead.'

She went on speaking into the phone. Her voice remained low, but the others in the room listened intently. 'No, he was found by a stranger,' they heard her say. 'A man whose car had broken down near the house, I believe . . . Yes, I'll tell him. I'll phone the inn. Will one of your cars be able to take him there when you've finished here? . . . Very well.'

Turning to face the company, Mrs Warwick announced, 'The police will be here as soon as they can in this fog. They'll have two cars, one of which will return right away to take this gentleman' — she gestured at Starkwedder — 'to the inn in the village. They want him to stay overnight and be available to talk to them tomorrow.'

'Well, since I can't leave with my car still in

the ditch, that's fine with me,' Starkwedder exclaimed. As he spoke, the door to the corridor opened, and a dark-haired man of medium height in his mid-forties entered the room, tying the cord of his dressing-gown. He suddenly stopped short just inside the door. 'Is something the matter, madam?' he asked, addressing Mrs Warwick. Then, glancing past her, he saw the body of Richard Warwick. 'Oh, my God,' he exclaimed.

'I'm afraid there's been a terrible tragedy, Angell,' Mrs Warwick replied. 'Mr Richard has been shot, and the police are on their way here.' Turning to Starkwedder, she said, 'This is Angell. He's — he was Richard's valet.'

The valet acknowledged Starkwedder's presence wth a slight, absent-minded bow. 'Oh, my God,' he repeated, as he continued to stare at the body of his late employer.

6

At eleven the following morning, Richard
Warwick's study looked somewhat more invit-
ing than it had on the previous foggy evening.
For one thing, the sun was shining on a cold,
clear, bright day, and the french windows
were wide open. The body had been removed
overnight, and the wheelchair had been pushed
into the recess, its former central place in the
room now occupied by the armchair. The
small table had been cleared of everything
except decanter and ashtray. A good-looking
young man in his twenties with short dark hair,
dressed in a tweed sports jacket and navy-
blue trousers, was sitting in the wheelchair,
reading a book of poems. After a few moments,
he got up. 'Beautiful,' he said to himself.
'Apposite and beautiful.' His voice was soft
and musical, with a pronounced Welsh accent.

The young man closed the book he had
been reading, and replaced it on the bookshelves in the recess. Then, after surveying the
room for a minute or two, he walked across to
the open french windows, and went out onto
the terrace. Almost immediately, a middle-
aged, thick-set, somewhat poker-faced man

carrying a briefcase entered the room from the hallway. Going to the armchair which faced out onto the terrace, he put his briefcase on it, and looked out of the windows. 'Sergeant Cadwallader!' he called sharply.

The younger man turned back into the room. 'Good morning, Inspector Thomas,' he said, and then continued, with a lilt in his voice, ''Season of mists and mellow fruitfulness, close bosom friend of the maturing sun'.'

The inspector, who had begun to unbutton his overcoat, stopped and looked intently at the young sergeant. 'I beg your pardon?' he asked, with a distinct note of sarcasm in his voice.

'That's Keats,' the sergeant informed him, sounding quite pleased with himself. The inspector responded with a baleful look at him, then shrugged, took off his coat, placed it on the wheelchair in the recess, and came back for his briefcase.

'You'd hardly credit the fine day it is,' Sergeant Cadwallader went on. 'When you think of the terrible time we had getting here last night. The worst fog I've known in years. 'The yellow fog that rubs its back upon the window-panes'. That's T.S. Eliot.' He waited for a reaction to his quotation from the inspector, but got none, so continued, 'It's no wonder the accidents piled up the way they did on the Cardiff road.'

'Might have been worse,' was his inspector's uninterested comment.

'I don't know about that,' said the sergeant, warming to his subject. 'At Porthcawl, that was a nasty smash. One killed and two children badly injured. And the mother crying her heart out there on the road. 'The pretty wretch left crying' — '

The inspector interrupted him. 'Have the fingerprint boys finished their job yet?' he asked.

Suddenly realizing that he had better get back to the business in hand, Sergeant Cadwallader replied, 'Yes, sir. I've got them all ready here for you.' He picked up a folder from the desk and opened it. The inspector sat in the desk chair and started to examine the first sheet of fingerprints in the folder. 'No trouble from the household about taking their prints?' he asked the sergeant casually.

'No trouble whatever,' the sergeant told him. 'Most obliging they were — anxious to help, as you might say. And that is only to be expected.'

'I don't know about that,' the inspector observed. 'I've usually found most people kick up no end of a fuss. Seem to think their prints are going to be filed in the Rogues'

Gallery.' He took a deep breath, stretching his arms, and continued to study the prints. 'Now, let's see. Mr Warwick — that's the deceased. Mrs Laura Warwick, his wife. Mrs Warwick senior, that's his mother. Young Jan Warwick, Miss Bennett and — who's this? Angle? Oh, Angell. Ah yes, that's his nurse-attendant, isn't it? And two other sets of prints. Let's see now — Hm. On outside of window, on decanter, on brandy glass overlaying prints of Richard Warwick and Angell and Mrs Laura Warwick, on cigarette lighter — and on the revolver. That will be that chap Michael Starkwedder. He gave Mrs Warwick brandy, and of course it was he who carried the gun in from the garden.'

Sergeant Cadwallader nodded slowly. 'Mr Starkwedder,' he growled, in a voice of deep suspicion.

The inspector, sounding amused, asked, 'You don't like him?'

'What's he doing here? That's what I'd like to know,' the sergeant replied. 'Running his car into a ditch and coming up to a house where there's been a murder done?'

The inspector turned in his chair to face his young colleague. 'You nearly ran our car into the ditch last night, coming up to a house where there'd been a murder done. And as to what he's doing here, he's been here — in this vicinity — for the last week, looking around for a small house or cottage.'

The sergeant looked unconvinced, and the inspector turned back to the desk, adding wryly, 'It seems he had a Welsh grandmother and he used to come here for holidays when he was a boy.'

Mollified, the sergeant conceded, 'Ah, well now, if he had a Welsh grandmother, that's a different matter, isn't it?' He raised his right arm and declaimed, '"One road leads to London, One road leads to Wales. My road leads me seawards, To the white dipping sails.' He was a fine poet, John Masefield. Very underrated.'

The inspector opened his mouth to complain, but then thought better of it and grinned instead. 'We ought to get the report on Starkwedder from Abadan any moment now,' he told the young sergeant. 'Have you got his prints for comparison?'

'I sent Jones round to the inn where he stayed last night,' Cadwallader informed his superior, 'but he'd gone out to the garage to see about getting his car salvaged. Jones rang the garage and spoke to him while he was there. He's been told to report at the station as soon as possible.'

'Right. Now, about this second set of unidentified prints. The print of a man's hand flat on the table by the body, and blurred impressions on both the outside and the inside of the french windows.'

'I'll bet that's MacGregor,' the sergeant exclaimed, snapping his fingers.

'Ye-es. Could be,' the inspector admitted reluctantly. 'But they weren't on the revolver. And you would think any man using a revolver to kill someone would have the sense enough to wear gloves, surely.'

'I don't know,' the sergeant observed. 'An unbalanced fellow like this MacGregor, deranged after the death of his child, he wouldn't think of that.'

'Well, we ought to get a description of MacGregor through from Norwich soon,' the inspector said.

The sergeant settled himself on the footstool. 'It's a sad story, whichever way you look at it,' he suggested. 'A man, his wife but lately dead, and his only child killed by furious driving.'

'If there'd been what you call furious driving,' the inspector corrected him impatiently, 'Richard Warwick would have got a sentence for manslaughter, or at any rate for the driving offence. In point of fact, his licence wasn't even endorsed.' He reached down to his briefcase, and took out the murder weapon.

'There is some fearful lying goes on

sometimes,' Sergeant Cadwallader muttered darkly. "'Lord, Lord, how this world is given to lying.' That's Shakespeare.'

His superior officer merely rose from the desk and looked at him. After a moment, the sergeant pulled himself together and rose to his feet. 'A man's hand flat on the table,' murmured the inspector as he went across to the table, taking the gun with him, and looking down at the table-top. 'I wonder.'

'Perhaps that could have been a guest in the house,' Sergeant Cadwallader suggested helpfully.

'Perhaps,' the inspector agreed. 'But I understand from Mrs Warwick that there were no visitors to the house yesterday. That manservant — Angell — might be able to tell us more. Go and fetch him, would you?'

'Yes, sir,' said Cadwallader as he went out. Left alone, the inspector spread out his own left hand on the table, and bent over the chair as if looking down at an invisible occupant. Then he went to the window and stepped outside, glancing both to left and right. He examined the lock of the french windows, and was turning back into the room when the sergeant returned, bringing with him Richard Warwick's valet-attendant, Angell, who was wearing a grey alpaca jacket, white shirt, dark tie and striped trousers.

'You're Henry Angell?' the inspector asked him.

'Yes, sir,' Angell replied.

'Sit down there, will you?' said the inspector.

Angell moved to sit on the sofa. 'Now then,' the inspector continued, 'you've been nurse-attendant and valet to Mr Richard Warwick — for how long?'

'For three and a half years, sir,' replied Angell. His manner was correct, but there was a shifty look in his eyes.

'Did you like the job?'

'I found it quite satisfactory, sir,' was Angell's reply.

'What was Mr Warwick like to work for?' the inspector asked him.

'Well, he was difficult.'

'But there were advantages, were there?'

'Yes, sir,' Angell admitted. 'I was extremely well paid.'

'And that made up for the other disadvantages, did it?' the inspector persisted.

'Yes, sir. I am trying to accumulate a little nest-egg.'

The inspector seated himself in the armchair, placing the gun on the table beside him. 'What were you doing before you came to Mr Warwick?' he asked Angell.

'The same sort of job, sir. I can show you

61

my references,' the valet replied. 'I've always given satisfaction, I hope. I've had some rather difficult employers — or patients, really. Sir James Walliston, for example. He is now a voluntary patient in a mental home. A *very* difficult person, sir.' He lowered his voice slightly before adding, 'Drugs!'

'Quite,' said the inspector. 'There was no question of drugs with Mr Warwick, I suppose?'

'No, sir. Brandy was what Mr Warwick liked to resort to.'

'Drank a lot of it, did he?' the inspector asked.

'Yes, sir,' Angell replied. 'He was a heavy drinker, but not an alcoholic, if you understand me. He never showed any ill-effects.'

The inspector paused before asking, 'Now, what's all this about guns and revolvers and — shooting at animals?'

'Well, it was his hobby, sir,' Angell told him. 'What we call in the profession a compensation. He'd been a big-game hunter in his day, I understand. Quite a little arsenal he's got in his bedroom there.' He nodded over his shoulder to indicate a room elsewhere in the house. 'Rifles, shotguns, air-guns, pistols and revolvers.'

'I see,' said the inspector. 'Well, now, just take a look at this gun here.'

Angell rose and stepped towards the table, then hesitated. 'It's all right,' the inspector told him, 'you needn't mind handling it.'

Angell picked up the gun, gingerly. 'Do you recognize it?' the inspector asked him.

'It's difficult to say, sir,' the valet replied. 'It looks like one of Mr Warwick's, but I don't really know very much about firearms. I can't say for certain which gun he had on the table beside him last night.'

'Didn't he have the same one every night?' asked the inspector.

'Oh, no, he had his fancies, sir,' said Angell. 'He kept using different ones.' The valet offered the gun back to the inspector, who took it.

'What was the good of his having a gun last night with all that fog?' queried the inspector.

'It was just a habit, sir,' Angell replied. 'He was used to it, as you might say.'

'All right, sit down again, would you?'

Angell sat again at one end of the sofa. The inspector examined the barrel of the gun before asking, 'When did you see Mr Warwick last?'

'About a quarter to ten last night, sir,' Angell told him. 'He had a bottle of brandy and a glass by his side, and the pistol he'd chosen. I arranged his rug for him, and wished him good-night.'

'Didn't he ever go to bed?' the inspector asked.

'No, sir,' replied the valet. 'At least, not in the usual sense of the term. He always slept in his chair. At six in the morning I would bring him tea, then I would wheel him into his bedroom, which had its own bathroom, where he'd bath and shave and so on, and then he'd usually sleep until lunch-time. I understand that he suffered from insomnia at night, and so he preferred to remain in his chair then. He was rather an eccentric gentleman.'

'And the window was shut when you left him?'

'Yes, sir,' Angell replied. 'There was a lot of fog about last night, and he didn't want it seeping into the house.'

'All right. The window was shut. Was it locked?'

'No, sir. That window was never locked.'

'So he could open it if he wanted to?'

'Oh, yes, sir. He had his wheelchair, you see. He could wheel himself over to the window and open it if the night should clear up.'

'I see.' The inspector thought for a moment, and then asked, 'You didn't hear a shot last night?'

'No, sir,' Angell replied.

The inspector walked across to the sofa

64

and looked down at Angell. 'Isn't that rather remarkable?' he asked.

'No, not really, sir,' was the reply. 'You see, my room is some distance away. Along a passage and through a baize door on the other side of the house.'

'Wasn't that rather awkward, in case your master wanted to summon you?'

'Oh no, sir,' said Angell. 'He had a bell that rang in my room.'

'But he didn't press that bell last night at all?'

'Oh no, sir,' Angell repeated. 'If he had done so, I would have woken up at once. It is, if I may say so, a very loud bell, sir.'

Inspector Thomas leaned forward on the arm of the sofa to approach Angell in another way.

'Did you — ' he began in a voice of controlled impatience, only to be interrupted by the shrill ring of the telephone. He waited for Sergeant Cadwallader to answer it, but the sergeant appeared to be dreaming with his eyes open and his lips moving soundlessly, perhaps immersed in some poetic reflection. After a moment, he realized that the inspector was staring at him, and that the phone was ringing. 'Sorry, sir, but a poem is on the way,' he explained as he went to the desk to answer the phone. 'Sergeant Cadwallader speaking,' he said. There was a pause, and then he added, 'Ah yes, indeed.' After another pause, he turned to the inspector. 'It's the police at Norwich, sir.'

Inspector Thomas took the phone from Cadwallader, and sat at the desk. 'Is that you, Edmundson?' he asked. 'Thomas here . . . Got it, right . . . Yes . . . Calgary, yes . . . Yes . . . Yes, the aunt, when did she die? . . . Oh, two months ago . . . Yes, I see . . . Eighteen, Thirty-fourth Street, Calgary.' He looked up impatiently at Cadwallader, and gestured to him to take a note of the address. 'Yes . . . Oh, it was, was it? . . . Yes, slowly please.' He looked meaningfully again at his sergeant. 'Medium height,' he repeated. 'Blue eyes, dark hair and beard . . . Yes, as you say, you remember the case . . . Ah, he did, did he? . . . Violent sort of fellow? . . . Yes . . . You're sending it along? Yes . . . Well, thank you, Edmundson. Tell me, what do you think, yourself? . . . Yes, yes, I know what the findings were, but what did *you* think yourself? . . . Ah, he had, had he? . . . Once or twice before . . . Yes, of course, you'd make some allowances . . . All right. Thanks.'

He replaced the receiver and said to the sergeant, 'Well, we've got some of the dope on MacGregor. It seems that, when his wife died, he travelled back to England from Canada to leave the child with an aunt of his

66

wife's who lived in North Walsham, because he had just got himself a job in Alaska and couldn't take the boy with him. Apparently he was terribly cut up at the child's death, and went about swearing revenge on Warwick. That's not uncommon after one of these accidents. Anyway, he went off back to Canada. They've got his address, and they'll send a cable off to Calgary. The aunt he was going to leave the child with died about two months ago.' He turned suddenly to Angell. 'You were there at the time, I suppose, Angell? Motor accident in North Walsham, running over a boy.'

'Oh yes, sir,' Angell replied. 'I remember it quite well.'

The inspector got up from the desk and went across to the valet. Seeing the desk chair empty, Sergeant Cadwallader promptly took the opportunity to sit down. 'What happened?' the inspector asked Angell. 'Tell me about the accident.'

'Mr Warwick was driving along the main street, and a little boy ran out of a house there,' Angell told him. 'Or it might have been the inn. I think it was. There was no chance of stopping. Mr Warwick ran over him before he could do a thing about it.'

'He was speeding, was he?' asked the inspector.

'Oh no, sir. That was brought out very clearly at the inquest. Mr Warwick was well within the speed limit.'

'I know that's what he said,' the inspector commented.

'It was quite true, sir,' Angell insisted. 'Nurse Warburton — a nurse Mr Warwick employed at the time — she was in the car, too, and she agreed.'

The inspector walked across to one end of the sofa. 'Did she happen to look at the speedometer at the time?' he queried.

'I believe Nurse Warburton did happen to see the speedometer,' Angell replied smoothly. 'She estimated that they were going at between twenty and twenty-five miles an hour. Mr Warwick was completely exonerated.'

'But the boy's father didn't agree?' the inspector asked.

'Perhaps that's only natural, sir,' was Angell's comment.

'Had Mr Warwick been drinking?'

Angell's reply was evasive. 'I believe he had had a glass of sherry, sir.' He and Inspector Thomas exchanged glances. Then the inspector crossed to the french windows, taking out his handkerchief and blowing his nose. 'Well, I think that'll do for now,' he told the valet.

Angell rose and went to the door. After a moment's hesitation, he turned back into the room. 'Excuse me, sir,' he said. 'But was Mr Warwick shot with his own gun?'

The inspector turned to him. 'That remains to be seen,' he observed. 'Whoever it was who shot him collided with Mr Starkwedder, who was coming up to the house to try to get help for his stranded vehicle. In the collision, the man dropped a gun. Mr Starkwedder picked it up — this gun.' He pointed to the gun on the table.

'I see, sir. Thank you, sir,' said Angell as he turned to the door again.

'By the way,' added the inspector, 'were there any visitors to the house yesterday? Yesterday evening in particular?'

Angell paused for just a moment, then eyed the inspector shiftily. 'Not that I can recall, sir — at present,' he replied. He left the room, closing the door behind him.

Inspector Thomas went back to the desk. 'If you ask me,' he said quietly to the sergeant, 'that fellow's a nasty bit of goods. Nothing you can put your finger on, but I don't like him.'

'I'm of the same opinion as you, regarding that,' Cadwallader replied. 'He's not a man I would trust, and what's more, I'd say there may have been something fishy about that accident.' Suddenly realizing that the inspector was standing over him, he got up quickly from his chair. The inspector took the notes Cadwallader had been making, and began to peruse them. 'Now I wonder if Angell knows something he hasn't told us about last night,' he began, and then broke off. 'Hello, what's this? ''Tis misty in November, But seldom in December.' That's not Keats, I hope?'

'No,' said Sergeant Cadwallader proudly. 'That's Cadwallader.'

7

The inspector thrust Cadwallader's notebook back at him roughly, as the door opened and Miss Bennett came in, closing the door carefully behind her. 'Inspector,' she said, 'Mrs Warwick is very anxious to see you. She is fussing a little.' She added quickly, 'I mean Mrs Warwick senior, Richard's mother. She doesn't admit it, but I don't think she's in the best of health, so please be gentle with her. Will you see her now?'

'Oh, certainly,' replied the inspector. 'Ask her to come in.'

Miss Bennett opened the door, beckoning, and Mrs Warwick came in. 'It's all right, Mrs Warwick,' the housekeeper assured her, leaving the room and shutting the door behind her.

'Good morning, madam,' the inspector said. Mrs Warwick did not return his greeting, but came directly to the point. 'Tell me, Inspector,' she ordered, 'what progress are you making?'

'It's rather early to say that, madam,' he replied, 'but you can rest assured that we're doing everything we can.'

Mrs Warwick sat on the sofa, placing her stick against the arm. 'This man MacGregor,' she asked. 'Has he been seen hanging about locally? Has anyone noticed him?'

'Enquiries have gone out about that,' the inspector informed her. 'But so far there's been no record of a stranger being seen in the locality.'

'That poor little boy,' Mrs Warwick continued. 'The one Richard ran over, I mean. I suppose it must have unhinged the father's brain. I know they told me he was very violent and abusive at the time. Perhaps that was only natural. But after two years! It seems incredible.'

'Yes,' the inspector agreed, 'it seems a long time to wait.'

'But he was a Scot, of course,' Mrs Warwick recalled. 'A MacGregor. A patient, dogged people, the Scots.'

'Indeed they are,' exclaimed Sergeant Cadwallader, forgetting himself and thinking out loud. ''There are few more impressive sights in the world than a Scotsman on the make,'' he continued, but the inspector immediately gave him a sharp look of disapproval, which quietened him.

'Your son had no preliminary warning?' Inspector Thomas asked Mrs Warwick. 'No threatening letter? Anything of that kind?'

'No, I'm sure he hadn't,' she replied quite firmly. 'Richard would have said so. He would have laughed about it.'

'He wouldn't have taken it seriously at all?' the inspector suggested.

'Richard always laughed at danger,' said Mrs Warwick. She sounded proud of her son.

'After the accident,' the inspector continued, 'did your son offer any compensation to the child's father?'

'Naturally,' Mrs Warwick replied. 'Richard was not a mean man. But it was refused. Indignantly refused, I may say.'

'Quite so,' murmured the inspector.

'I understand MacGregor's wife was dead,' Mrs Warwick recalled. 'The boy was all he had in the world. It was a tragedy, really.'

'But in your opinion it was not your son's fault?' the inspector asked. When Mrs Warwick did not answer, he repeated his question. 'I said — it was not your son's fault?'

She remained silent a moment longer before replying, 'I heard you.'

'Perhaps you don't agree?' the inspector persisted.

Mrs Warwick turned away on the sofa, embarrassed, fingering a cushion. 'Richard drank too much,' she said finally. 'And of course he'd been drinking that day.'

'A glass of sherry?' the inspector prompted her.

'A glass of sherry!' Mrs Warwick repeated with a bitter laugh. 'He'd been drinking pretty heavily. He did drink — very heavily. That decanter there — ' She indicated the decanter on the table near the armchair in the french windows. 'That decanter was filled every evening, and it was always practically empty in the morning.'

Sitting on the stool and facing Mrs Warwick, the inspector said to her, quietly, 'So you think that your son was to blame for the accident?'

'Of course he was to blame,' she replied. 'I've never had the least doubt of it.'

'But he was exonerated,' the inspector reminded her.

Mrs Warwick laughed. 'That nurse who was in the car with him? That Warburton woman?' she snorted. 'She was a fool, and she was devoted to Richard. I expect he paid her pretty handsomely for her evidence, too.'

'Do you actually know that?' the inspector asked, sharply.

Mrs Warwick's tone was equally sharp as she replied, 'I don't know anything, but I arrive at my own conclusions.'

The inspector went across to Sergeant Cadwallader and took his notes from him,

74

while Mrs Warwick continued. 'I'm telling you all this now,' she said, 'because what you want is the truth, isn't it? You want to be sure there's sufficient incentive for murder on the part of that little boy's father. Well, in my opinion, there was. Only, I didn't think that after all this time — ' Her voice trailed away into silence.

The inspector looked up from the notes he had been consulting. 'You didn't hear anything last night?' he asked her.

'I'm a little deaf, you know,' Mrs Warwick replied quickly. 'I didn't know anything was wrong until I heard people talking and passing my door. I came down, and young Jan said, 'Richard's been shot. Richard's been shot.' I thought at first — ' She passed her hand over her eyes. 'I thought it was a joke of some kind.'

'Jan is your younger son?' the inspector asked her.

'He's not *my* son,' Mrs Warwick replied. The inspector looked at her quickly as she went on, 'I divorced my husband many years ago. He remarried. Jan is the son of the second marriage.' She paused, then continued. 'It sounds more complicated than it is, really. When both his parents died, the boy came here. Richard and Laura had just been married then. Laura has always been very

75

kind to Richard's half-brother. She's been like an elder sister to him, really.'

She paused, and the inspector took the opportunity to lead her back to talking about Richard Warwick. 'Yes, I see,' he said, 'but now, about your son Richard — '

'I loved my son, Inspector,' Mrs Warwick said, 'but I was not blind to his faults, and they were very largely due to the accident that made him a cripple. He was a proud man, an outdoor man, and to have to live the life of an invalid and a semi-cripple was very galling to him. It did not, shall we say, improve his character.'

'Yes, I see,' observed the inspector. 'Would you say his married life was happy?'

'I haven't the least idea.' Mrs Warwick clearly had no intention of saying any more on the subject. 'Is there anything else you wish to know, Inspector?' she asked.

'No thank you, Mrs Warwick,' Inspector Thomas replied. 'But I should like to talk to Miss Bennett now, if I may.'

Mrs Warwick rose, and Sergeant Cadwallader went to open the door for her. 'Yes, of course,' she said. 'Miss Bennett. Benny, we call her. She's the person who can help you most. She's so practical and efficient.'

'She's been with you for a long time?' the inspector asked.

'Oh yes, for years and years. She looked after Jan when he was little, and before that she helped with Richard, too. Oh, yes, she's looked after all of us. A very faithful person, Benny.' Acknowledging the sergeant at the door with a nod, she left the room.

8

Sergeant Cadwallader closed the door and stood with his back against it, looking at the inspector. 'So Richard Warwick was a drinking man, eh?' he commented. 'You know, I've heard that said of him before. And all those pistols and air-guns and rifles. A little queer in the head, if you ask me.'

'Could be,' Inspector Thomas replied laconically.

The telephone rang. Expecting his sergeant to answer it, the inspector looked meaningfully at him, but Cadwallader had become immersed in his notes as he strolled across to the armchair and sat, completely oblivious of the phone. After a while, realizing that the sergeant's mind was elsewhere, no doubt in the process of composing a poem, the inspector sighed, crossed to the desk, and picked up the receiver.

'Hello,' he said. 'Yes, speaking . . . Starkwedder, he came in? He gave you his prints? . . . Good . . . yes — well, ask him to wait . . . yes, I shall be back in half an hour or so . . . yes, I want to ask him some more questions . . . Yes, goodbye.'

Towards the end of this conversation, Miss Bennett had entered the room, and was standing by the door. Noticing her, Sergeant Cadwallader rose from his armchair and took up a position behind it. 'Yes?' said Miss Bennett with an interrogative inflection. She addressed the inspector. 'You want to ask me some questions? I've got a good deal to do this morning.'

'Yes, Miss Bennett,' the inspector replied. 'I want to hear your account of the car accident with the child in Norfolk.'

'The MacGregor child?'

'Yes, the MacGregor child. You remembered his name very quickly last night, I hear.'

Miss Bennett turned to close the door behind her. 'Yes,' she agreed. 'I have a very good memory for names.'

'And no doubt,' the inspector continued, 'the occurrence made some impression on you. But you weren't in the car yourself, were you?'

Miss Bennett seated herself on the sofa. 'No, no, I wasn't in the car,' she told him. 'It was the hospital nurse Mr Warwick had at the time. A Nurse Warburton.'

'Did you go to the inquest?' the inspector asked.

'No,' she replied. 'But Richard told us about it when he came back. He said the boy's father had threatened him, had said he'd get even with him. We didn't take it seriously, of course.'

Inspector Thomas came closer to her. 'Had you formed any particular impression about the accident?' he asked.

'I don't know what you mean.'

The inspector regarded Miss Bennett for a moment, and then said, 'I mean do you think it happened because Mr Warwick had been drinking?'

She made a dismissive gesture. 'Oh, I suppose his mother told you that,' she snorted. 'Well, you mustn't go by all she says. She's got a prejudice against drink. Her husband — Richard's father — drank.'

'You think, then,' the inspector suggested to her, 'that Richard Warwick's account was true, that he was driving well within the speed limit, and that the accident could not have been avoided?'

'I don't see why it shouldn't have been the truth,' Miss Bennett insisted. 'Nurse Warburton corroborated his evidence.'

'And her word was to be relied upon?'

Clearly taking exception to what she seemed to regard as an aspersion on her profession, Miss Bennett said with some asperity, 'I should hope so. After all, people don't go around telling lies — not about that sort of thing. Do they?'

Sergeant Cadwallader, who had been following the questioning, now broke in. 'Oh, do they not, indeed!' he exclaimed. 'The way they talk sometimes, you'd think that not only were they within the speed limit, but that they'd managed to get into reverse at the same time!'

Annoyed at this latest interruption, the inspector turned slowly and looked at the sergeant. Miss Bennett also regarded the young man in some surprise. Embarrassed, Sergeant Cadwallader looked down at his notes, and the inspector turned again to Miss Bennett. 'What I'm getting at is this,' he told her. 'In the grief and stress of the moment, a man might easily threaten revenge for an accident that had killed his child. But on reflection, if things were as stated, he would surely have realized that the accident was not Richard Warwick's fault.'

'Oh,' said Miss Bennett. 'Yes, I see what you mean.'

The inspector paced slowly about the room as he continued, 'If, on the other hand, the car had been driven erratically and at excessive speed — if the car had been, shall we say, out of control — '

'Did Laura tell you that?' Miss Bennett interrupted him.

81

The inspector turned to look at her, surprised at her mention of the murdered man's wife. 'What makes you think she told me?' he asked.

'I don't know,' Miss Bennett replied. 'I just wondered.' Looking confused, she glanced at her watch. 'Is that all?' she asked. 'I'm very busy this morning.' She walked to the door, opened it, and was about to leave when the inspector said, 'I'd like to have a word with young Jan next, if I may.'

Miss Bennett turned in the doorway. 'Oh, he's rather excited this morning,' she said, sounding somewhat truculent. 'I'd really be much obliged if you wouldn't talk to him — raking it all up. I've just got him calmed down.'

'I'm sorry, but I'm afraid we must ask him a few questions,' the inspector insisted.

Miss Bennett closed the door firmly and came back into the room. 'Why can't you just find this man MacGregor, and question him?' she suggested. 'He can't have got far away.'

'We'll find him. Don't you worry,' the inspector assured her.

'I hope you will,' Miss Bennett retorted. 'Revenge, indeed! Why, it's not Christian.'

'Of course,' the inspector agreed, adding meaningfully, 'especially when the accident was not Mr Warwick's fault and could not have been avoided.'

Miss Bennett gave him a sharp look. There was a pause, and then the inspector repeated, 'I'd like to speak to Jan, please.'

'I don't know if I can find him,' said Miss Bennett. 'He may have gone out.' She left the room quickly. The inspector looked at Sergeant Cadwallader, nodding his head towards the door, and the sergeant followed her out. In the corridor, Miss Bennett admonished Cadwallader. 'You're not to worry him,' she said. She came back into the room. 'You're not to worry the boy,' she ordered the inspector. 'He's very easily — unsettled. He gets excited, temperamental.'

The inspector regarded her silently for a moment, and then asked, 'Is he ever violent?'

'No, of course not. He's a very sweet boy, very gentle. Docile, really. I simply meant that you might upset him. It's not good for children, things like murder. And that's all he is, really. A child.'

The inspector sat in the chair at the desk. 'You needn't worry, Miss Bennett, I assure you,' he told her. 'We quite understand the position.'

9

Just then, Sergeant Cadwallader ushered in Jan, who rushed up to the inspector. 'Do you want me?' he cried excitedly. 'Have you caught him yet? Will there be blood on his clothes?'

'Now, Jan,' Miss Bennett cautioned him, 'you must behave yourself. Just answer any questions the gentleman asks you.'

Jan turned happily to Miss Bennett, and then back to the inspector. 'Oh, yes, I will,' he promised. 'But can't I ask any questions?'

'Of course you can ask questions,' the inspector assured him kindly.

Miss Bennett sat on the sofa. 'I'll wait while you're talking to him,' she said.

The inspector got up quickly, went to the door and opened it invitingly. 'No thank you, Miss Bennett,' he said firmly. 'We shan't need you. And didn't you say you're rather busy this morning?'

'I'd rather stay,' she insisted.

'I'm sorry.' The inspector's voice was sharp. 'We always like to talk to people one at a time.'

Miss Bennett looked at the inspector and

then at Sergeant Cadwallader. Realizing that she was defeated, she gave a snort of annoyance and swept out of the room, the inspector closing the door after her. The sergeant moved to the alcove, preparing to take more notes, while Inspector Thomas sat on the sofa. 'I don't suppose,' he said amiably to Jan, 'that you've ever been in close contact with a murder before, have you?'

'No, no, I haven't,' Jan replied eagerly. 'It's very exciting, isn't it?' He knelt on the footstool. 'Have you got any clues — finger-prints or bloodstains or anything?'

'You seem very interested in blood,' the inspector observed with a friendly smile.

'Oh, I am,' Jan replied, quietly and seriously. 'I like blood. It's a beautiful colour, isn't it? That nice clear red.' He too sat down on the sofa, laughing nervously. 'Richard shot things, you know, and then they used to bleed. It's really very funny, isn't it? I mean it's funny that Richard, who was always shooting things, should have been shot himself. Don't you think that's funny?'

The inspector's voice was quiet, his inflection rather dry, as he replied, 'I suppose it has its humorous side.' He paused. 'Are you very upset that your brother — your half-brother, I mean — is dead?'

'Upset?' Jan sounded surprised. 'That

Richard is dead? No, why should I be?'

'Well, I thought perhaps you were — very fond of him,' the inspector suggested.

'Fond of him!' exclaimed Jan in what sounded like genuine astonishment. 'Fond of Richard? Oh, no, nobody could be *fond* of Richard.'

'I suppose his wife was fond of him, though,' the inspector urged.

A look of surprise passed across Jan's face. 'Laura?' he exclaimed. 'No, I don't think so. She was always on *my* side.'

'On your side?' the inspector asked. 'What does that mean, exactly?'

Jan suddenly looked scared. 'Yes. Yes,' he almost shouted, hurriedly. 'When Richard wanted to have me sent away.'

'Sent away?' the inspector prompted him gently.

'To one of those places,' the youngster explained. 'You know, where they send you, and you're locked up, and you can't get out. He said Laura would come and see me, perhaps, sometimes.' Jan shook a little, then rose, backed away from the inspector, and looked across at Sergeant Cadwallader. 'I wouldn't like to be locked up,' he continued, his voice now tremulous. 'I'd hate to be locked up.'

He stood at the french windows, looking

out onto the terrace. 'I like things open, always,' he called out to them. 'I like my window open, and my door, so that I can be sure I can get out.' He turned back into the room. 'But nobody can lock me up *now*, can they?'

'No, lad,' the inspector assured him. 'I shouldn't think so.'

'Not now that Richard's dead,' Jan added. Momentarily, he sounded almost smug.

The inspector got up and moved round the sofa. 'So Richard wanted you locked up?' he asked.

'Laura says he only said it to tease me,' Jan told him. 'She said that was all it was, and she said it was all right, and that as long as she was here she'd make quite sure that I would never be locked up.' He went to perch on one arm of the armchair. 'I love Laura,' he continued, speaking with a nervous excitement. 'I love Laura a terrible lot. We have wonderful times together, you know. We look for butter-flies and birds' eggs, and we play games together. Bezique. Do you know that game? It's a clever one. And Beggar-my-neighbour. Oh, it's great fun doing things with Laura.'

The inspector went across to lean on the other arm of the chair. His voice had a kindly tone to it as he asked, 'I don't suppose you remember anything about this accident that happened when you were living in Norfolk, do you? When a little boy got run over?'

'Oh, yes, I remember that,' Jan replied quite cheerfully. 'Richard went to the inquest.'

'Yes, that's right. What else do you remember?' the inspector encouraged him.

'We had salmon for lunch that day,' Jan said immediately. 'Richard and Warby came back together. Warby was a bit flustered, but Richard was laughing.'

'Warby?' the inspector queried. 'Is that Nurse Warburton?'

'Yes, Warby. I didn't like her much. But Richard was so pleased with her that day that he kept saying, 'Jolly good show, Warby.''

The door suddenly opened, and Laura Warwick appeared. Sergeant Cadwallader went across to her, and Jan called out, 'Hello, Laura.'

'Am I interrupting?' Laura asked the inspector.

'No, of course not, Mrs Warwick,' he replied. 'Do sit down, won't you?'

Laura came further into the room, and the sergeant shut the door behind her. 'Is — is Jan — ?' Laura began. She paused.

'I'm just asking him,' the inspector explained, 'if he remembers anything about that accident to the boy in Norfolk. The MacGregor boy.'

Laura sat at the end of the sofa. 'Do you remember, Jan?' she asked him.

'Of course I remember,' the lad replied, eagerly. 'I remember everything.' He turned to the inspector. 'I've told you, haven't I?' he asked.

The inspector did not reply to him directly. Instead, he moved slowly to the sofa and, addressing Laura Warwick, asked, 'What do you know about the accident, Mrs Warwick? Was it discussed at luncheon that day, when your husband came back from the inquest?'

'I don't remember,' Laura replied immediately.

Jan rose quickly and moved towards her. 'Oh, yes, you do, Laura, surely,' he reminded her. 'Don't you remember Richard saying that one brat more or less in the world didn't make any difference?'

Laura rose. 'Please — ' she implored the inspector.

'It's quite all right, Mrs Warwick,' Inspector Thomas assured her gently. 'It's important, you know, that we get at the truth of that accident. After all, presumably it's the motive for what happened here last night.'

'Oh yes,' she sighed. 'I know. I know.'

'According to your mother-in-law,' the inspector continued, 'your husband had been drinking that day.'

'I expect he had,' Laura admitted. 'It — it wouldn't surprise me.'

The inspector moved to sit at the end of the sofa. 'Did you actually see or meet this man, MacGregor?' he asked her.

'No,' said Laura. 'No, I didn't go to the inquest.'

'He seems to have felt very revengeful,' the inspector commented.

Laura gave a sad smile. 'It must have affected his brain, I think,' she agreed.

Jan, who had gradually been getting very excited, came up to them. 'If I had an enemy,' he exclaimed aggressively, 'that's what I'd do. I'd wait a long time, and then I'd come creeping along in the dark with my gun. Then — ' He shot at the armchair with an imaginary gun. 'Bang, bang, bang.'

'Be quiet, Jan,' Laura ordered him, sharply.

Jan suddenly looked upset. 'Are you angry with me, Laura?' he asked her, childishly.

'No, darling,' Laura reassured him, 'I'm not angry. But try not to get too excited.'

'I'm not excited,' Jan insisted.

10

Crossing the front hall, Miss Bennett paused to admit Starkwedder and a police constable who seemed to have arrived on the doorstep together.

'Good morning, Miss Bennett,' Starkwedder greeted her. 'I'm here to see Inspector Thomas.'

Miss Bennett nodded. 'Good morning — oh, good morning, Constable. They're in the study, both of them — I don't know what's going on.'

'Good morning, madam,' the police constable replied. 'I've brought these for the inspector. Perhaps Sergeant Cadwallader could take them.'

'What's this?' Laura asked, over the rumble of voices outside.

The inspector rose and moved towards the door. 'It sounds as if Mr Starkwedder is back.'

As Starkwedder entered the room, Sergeant Cadwallader went out into the hall to deal with the constable. Meanwhile, young Jan sank into the armchair, and observed the proceedings eagerly.

'Look here,' exclaimed Starkwedder as he came into the room. 'I can't spend all day kicking my heels at the police station. I've given you my fingerprints, and then I insisted that they bring me along here. I've got things to do. I've got two appointments with a house agent today.' He suddenly noticed Laura. 'Oh — good morning, Mrs Warwick,' he greeted her. 'I'm terribly sorry about what has happened.'

'Good morning,' Laura replied, distantly.

The inspector went across to the table by the armchair. 'Last night, Mr Starkwedder,' he asked, 'did you by any chance lay your hand on this table, and subsequently push the window open?'

Starkwedder joined him at the table. 'I don't know,' he admitted. 'I could have done. Is it important? I can't remember.'

Sergeant Cadwallader came back into the room, carrying a file. After shutting the door behind him, he walked across to the inspector. 'Here are Mr Starkwedder's prints, sir,' he reported. 'The constable brought them. And the ballistics report.'

'Ah, let's see,' said the inspector. 'The bullet that killed Richard Warwick definitely came from this gun. As for the fingerprints, well, we'll soon see.' He went to the chair by the desk, sat, and began to study the

92

documents, while the sergeant moved into the alcove.

After a pause, Jan, who had been staring intently at Starkwedder, asked him, 'You've just come back from Abadan, haven't you? What's Abadan like?'

'It's hot,' was the only response he got from Starkwedder, who then turned to Laura. 'How are you today, Mrs Warwick?' he asked. 'Are you feeling better?'

'Oh yes, thank you,' Laura replied. 'I've got over the shock now.'

'Good,' said Starkwedder.

The inspector had risen, and now approached Starkwedder on the sofa. 'Your prints,' he announced, 'are on the window, decanter, glass and cigarette lighter. The prints on the table are not yours. They're a completely unidentified set of prints.' He looked around the room. 'That settles it, then,' he continued. 'Since there were no visitors here — ' he paused and looked at Laura — 'last night — ?'

'No,' Laura assured him.

'Then they must be MacGregor's,' continued the inspector.

'MacGregor's?' asked Starkwedder, looking at Laura.

'You sound surprised,' said the inspector.

'Yes — I am, rather,' Starkwedder admitted. 'I mean, I should have expected him to

93

have worn gloves.'

The inspector nodded. 'You're right,' he agreed. 'He handled the revolver with gloves.'

'Was there any quarrel?' Starkwedder asked, addressing his question to Laura Warwick. 'Or was nothing heard but the shot?'

It was with an effort that Laura replied, 'I — we — Benny and I, that is — we just heard the shot. But then, we wouldn't have heard anything from upstairs.'

Sergeant Cadwallader had been gazing out at the garden through the small window in the alcove. Now, seeing someone approaching across the lawn, he moved to one side of the french windows. In through the windows there entered a handsome man in his mid-thirties, above medium height, with fair hair, blue eyes and a somewhat military aspect. He paused at the entrance, looking very worried. Jan, the first of the others in the room to notice him, squealed excitedly, 'Julian! Julian!'

The newcomer looked at Jan and then turned to Laura Warwick. 'Laura!' he exclaimed. 'I've just heard. I'm — I'm most terribly sorry.'

'Good morning, Major Farrar,' Inspector Thomas greeted him.

Julian Farrar turned to the inspector. 'This is an extraordinary business.' he said. 'Poor Richard.'

'He was lying here in his wheelchair,' Jan

told Farrar excitedly. 'He was all crumpled up. And there was a piece of paper on his chest. Do you know what it said? It said 'Paid in full'.'

'Yes. There, there, Jan,' Julian Farrar murmured, patting the boy's shoulder.

'It *is* exciting, isn't it?' Jan continued, looking eagerly at him.

Farrar moved past him. 'Yes. Yes, of course it's exciting,' he assured Jan, looking enquiringly towards Starkwedder as he spoke.

The inspector introduced the two men to each other. 'This is Mr Starkwedder — Major Farrar, who may be our next Member of Parliament. He's contesting the by-election.'

Starkwedder and Julian Farrar shook hands, politely murmuring, 'How do you do?' The inspector moved away, beckoning to the sergeant who joined him. They conferred, as Starkwedder explained to Major Farrar, 'I'd run my car into a ditch, and I was coming up to the house to see if I could telephone and get some help. A man dashed out of the house, almost knocking me over.'

'But which way did this man go?' Farrar asked.

'No idea,' Starkwedder replied. 'He vanished into the mist like a conjuring trick.' He turned away, while Jan, kneeling in the armchair and looking expectantly at Farrar, said, 'You told Richard someone would shoot him one day, didn't you, Julian?'

There was a pause. Everyone in the room looked at Julian Farrar.

Farrar thought for a moment. Then, 'Did I? I don't remember,' he said brusquely.

'Oh, yes, you did,' Jan insisted. 'At dinner one night. You know, you and Richard were having a sort of argument, and you said, 'One of these days, Richard, somebody'll put a bullet through your head.''

'A remarkable prophecy,' the inspector commented.

Julian Farrar moved to sit on one end of the footstool. 'Oh well,' he said, 'Richard and his guns were pretty fair nuisance value, you know. People didn't like it. Why, there was that fellow — you remember, Laura? Your gardener, Griffiths. You know — the one Richard sacked. Griffiths certainly said to me — and on more than one occasion — 'One of these days, look you, I shall come with my gun and I shall shoot Mr Warwick.''

'Oh, Griffiths wouldn't do a thing like that,' Laura exclaimed quickly.

Farrar looked contrite. 'No, no, of course not,' he admitted. 'I — I didn't mean that. I mean that it was the sort of thing that — er — people said about Richard.'

To cover his embarrassment, he took out

his cigarette-case and extracted a cigarette.

The inspector sat in the desk chair, looking thoughtful. Starkwedder stood in a corner near the alcove, close to Jan who gazed at him with interest.

'I wish I'd come over here last night,' Julian Farrar announced, addressing no one in particular. 'I meant to.'

'But that awful fog,' Laura said quietly. 'You couldn't come out in that.'

'No,' Farrar replied. 'I had my committee members over to dine with me. When they found the fog coming on, they went home rather early. I thought then of coming along to see you, but I decided against it.' Searching in his pockets, he asked, 'Has anyone got a match? I seem to have mislaid my lighter.'

He looked around, and suddenly noticed the lighter on the table where Laura had left it the night before. Rising, he went across to pick it up, observed by Starkwedder. 'Oh, here it is,' said Farrar. 'Couldn't imagine where I'd left it.'

'Julian — ' Laura began.

'Yes?' Farrar offered her a cigarette, and she took one. 'I'm most awfully sorry about all this, Laura,' he said. 'If there's anything I can do — ' His voice trailed off indecisively.

'Yes. Yes, I know,' Laura replied, as Farrar lit their cigarettes.

Jan suddenly spoke, addressing Starkwedder. 'Can you shoot, Mr Starkwedder?' he asked. 'I can, you know. Richard used to let me try, sometimes. Of course, I wasn't as good as he was.'

'Did he, indeed?' said Starkwedder, turning to Jan. 'What sort of gun did he let you use?'

As Jan engaged Starkwedder's attention, Laura took the opportunity of speaking quickly to Julian Farrar.

'Julian, I must talk to you. I must,' she murmured softly.

Farrar's voice was equally low. 'Careful,' he warned her.

'It was a .22,' Jan was telling Starkwedder. 'I'm quite good at shooting, aren't I, Julian?' He went across to Julian Farrar. 'Do you remember the time you took me to the fair? I knocked two of the bottles down, didn't I?'

'You did indeed, my lad,' Farrar assured him. 'You've got a good eye, that's what counts. Good eye for a cricket ball, too. That was quite a sensational game, that match we had last summer,' he added.

Jan smiled at him happily, and then sat on the footstool, looking across at the inspector who was now examining documents on the desk. There was a pause. Then Starkwedder, as he took out a cigarette, asked Laura, 'Do you mind if I smoke?'

'Of course not,' replied Laura.

Starkwedder turned to Julian Farrar. 'May I borrow your lighter?'

'Of course,' said Farrar. 'Here it is.'

'Ah, a nice lighter, this,' Starkwedder commented, lighting his cigarette.

Laura made a sudden movement, and then stopped herself. 'Yes,' Farrar said carelessly. 'It works better than most.'

'Rather — distinctive,' Starkwedder observed. He gave a quick glance at Laura, and then returned the lighter to Julian Farrar with a murmured word of thanks.

Jan left his footstool, and stood behind the inspector's chair. 'Richard has lots of guns,' he confided. 'Air-guns, too. And he's got one gun that he used to use in Africa to shoot elephants. Would you like to see them? They're in Richard's bedroom through there.' He pointed the way.

'All right,' said the inspector, rising. 'You show them to us.' He smiled at Jan, adding genially, 'You know, you're being very helpful to us. Helping us quite a lot. We ought to take you into the police force.'

Putting a hand on the boy's shoulder, he steered him towards the door, which the sergeant opened for them. 'We don't need to keep you, Mr Starkwedder,' the inspector called from the door. 'You can go about your business now. Just keep in touch with us, that's all.'

'All right,' replied Starkwedder, as Jan, the inspector and the sergeant left the room, the sergeant closing the door behind them.

11

There was an awkward pause after the police officers had left the room with Jan. Then Starkwedder remarked, 'Well, I suppose I'd better go and see whether they've managed to get my car out of the ditch yet. We didn't seem to pass it on the way here.'

'No,' Laura explained. 'The drive comes up from the other road.'

'Yes, I see,' Starkwedder answered, as he walked across to the french windows. He turned. 'How different things look in the daylight,' he observed as he stepped out onto the terrace.

As soon as he had gone, Laura and Julian Farrar turned to each other. 'Julian!' Laura exclaimed. 'That lighter! I said it was *mine*.'

'You said it was yours? To the inspector?' Farrar asked.

'No. To *him*.'

'To — to this fellow — ' Farrar began, and then stopped as they both noticed Starkwedder walking along the terrace outside the windows. 'Laura — ' he began again.

'Be careful,' said Laura, going across to the little window in the alcove and looking out. 'He may be listening to us.'

'Who is he?' asked Farrar. 'Do you know him?'

Laura came back to the centre of the room. 'No. No, I don't know him,' she told Farrar. 'He — he had an accident with his car, and he came here last night. Just after — '

Julian Farrar touched her hand which rested on the back of the sofa. 'It's all right, Laura. You know that I'll do everything I can.'

'Julian — *fingerprints*,' Laura gasped.

'What fingerprints?'

'On that table. On that table there, and on the pane of glass. Are they — yours?'

Farrar removed his hand from hers, indicating that Starkwedder was again walking along the terrace outside. Without turning to the window, Laura moved away from him, saying loudly, 'It's very kind of you, Julian, and I'm sure there will be a lot of business things you can help us with.'

Starkwedder was pacing about, outside on the terrace. When he had moved out of sight, Laura turned to face Julian Farrar again. 'Are those fingerprints yours, Julian? Think.'

Farrar considered for a moment. Then, 'On the table — yes — they might have been.'

'Oh God!' Laura cried. 'What shall we do?'

Starkwedder could now be glimpsed again, walking back and forth along the terrace just outside the windows. Laura puffed at her cigarette. 'The police think it's a man called MacGregor — ' she told Julian. She gave him a desperate look, pausing to allow him an opportunity to make some comment.

'Well, that's all right, then,' he replied. 'They'll probably go on thinking so.'

'But suppose — ' Laura began.

Farrar interrupted her. 'I must go,' he said. 'I've got an appointment.' He rose. 'It's all right, Laura,' he said, patting her shoulder. 'Don't worry. I'll see that you're all right.'

The look on Laura's face was one of an incomprehension verging on desperation. Apparently oblivious of it, Farrar walked across to the french windows. As he pushed a window open, Starkwedder was approaching with the obvious intention of entering the room. Farrar politely moved aside, to avoid colliding with him.

'Oh, are you off now?' Starkwedder asked him.

'Yes,' said Farrar. 'Things are rather busy these days. Election coming on, you know, in a week's time.'

'Oh, I see,' Starkwedder replied. 'Excuse my ignorance, but what are you? Tory?'

'I'm a Liberal,' said Farrar. He sounded slightly indignant.

'Oh, are they still at it?' Starkwedder asked, brightly.

Julian Farrar drew a sharp breath, and left the room without another word. When he had gone, not quite slamming the door behind him, Starkwedder looked at Laura almost fiercely. Then, 'I see,' he said, his anger rising. 'Or at least I'm beginning to see.'

'What do you mean?' Laura asked him.

'That's the boyfriend, isn't it?' He came closer to her. 'Well, come on now, is it?'

'Since you ask,' Laura replied, defiantly, 'yes, it is!'

Starkwedder looked at her for a moment without speaking. Then, 'There are quite a few things you didn't tell me last night, aren't there?' he said angrily. 'That's why you snatched up his lighter in such a hurry and said it was yours.' He walked away a few paces and then turned to face her again. 'And how long has this been going on between you and him?'

'For quite some time now,' Laura said quietly.

'But you didn't ever decide to leave Warwick and go away together?'

'No,' Laura answered. 'There's Julian's career, for one thing. It might ruin him politically.'

Starkwedder sat himself down ill-temperedly at one end of the sofa. 'Oh, surely not, these days,' he snapped. 'Don't they all take adultery in their stride?'

'These would have been special circumstances,' Laura tried to explain. 'He was a friend of Richard's, and with Richard being a cripple — '

'Oh yes, I see. It certainly wouldn't have been good publicity!' Starkwedder retorted.

Laura came over to the sofa and stood looking down at him. 'I suppose you think I ought to have told you this last night?' she observed, icily.

Starkwedder looked away from her. 'You were under no obligation,' he muttered.

Laura seemed to relent. 'I didn't think it mattered — ' she began. 'I mean — all I could think of was my having shot Richard.'

Starkwedder seemed to warm to her again, as he murmured, 'Yes, yes, I see.' After a pause, he added, '*I* couldn't think of anything else, either.' He paused again, and then looked up at her. 'Do you want to try a little experiment?' he asked. 'Where were you standing when you shot Richard?'

'Where was I standing?' Laura echoed. She sounded perplexed.

'That's what I said.'

After a moment's thought, Laura replied, 'Oh — over there.' She nodded vaguely towards the french windows.

'Go and stand where you were standing,' Starkwedder instructed her.

Laura rose and began to move nervously about the room. 'I — I can't remember,' she told him. 'Don't ask me to remember.' She sounded scared now. 'I — I was upset. I — '

Starkwedder interrupted her. 'Your husband said something to you,' he reminded her. 'Something that made you snatch up the gun.'

Rising from the sofa, he went to the table by the armchair and put his cigarette out. 'Well, come on, let's act it out,' he continued. 'There's the table, there's the gun.' He took Laura's cigarette from her, and put it in the ashtray. 'Now then, you were quarrelling. You picked up the gun — pick it up — '

'I don't want to!' Laura cried.

'Don't be a little fool,' Starkwedder growled. 'It's not loaded. Come on, pick it up. Pick it up.'

Laura picked up the gun, hesitantly.

'You snatched it up,' he reminded her. 'You didn't pick it up gingerly like that. You snatched it up, and you shot him. Show me how you did it.'

Holding the gun awkwardly, Laura backed away from him. 'I — I — ' she began.

'Go on. Show me,' Starkwedder shouted at her.

Laura tried to aim the gun. 'Go on, shoot!' he repeated, still shouting. 'It isn't loaded.'

When she still hesitated, he snatched the gun from her in triumph. 'I thought so,' he exclaimed. 'You've never fired a revolver in your life. You don't know how to do it.' Looking at the gun, he continued, 'You don't even know enough to release the safety catch.'

He dropped the gun on the footstool, then walked to the back of the sofa, and turned to face her. After a pause, he said quietly, 'You didn't shoot your husband.'

'I did,' Laura insisted.

'Oh no, you didn't,' Starkwedder repeated with conviction.

Sounding frightened, Laura asked, 'Then why should I say I did?'

Starkwedder took a deep breath and then exhaled. Coming round the sofa, he threw himself down on it heavily. 'The answer to that seems pretty obvious to me. Because it was Julian Farrar who shot him,' he retorted.

'No!' Laura exclaimed, almost shouting.

'Yes!'

'No!' she repeated.

'I say yes,' he insisted.

'If it was Julian,' Laura asked him, 'why on earth should I say *I* did it?'

Starkwedder looked at her levelly. 'Because,' he said, 'you thought — and thought quite rightly — that I'd cover up for *you*. Oh yes, you were certainly right about that.' He lounged back into the sofa before continuing, 'Yes, you played me along very prettily. But I'm through, do you hear? I'm through. I'm damned if I'm going to tell a pack of lies to save Major Julian Farrar's skin.'

There was a pause. For a few moments Laura said nothing. Then she smiled and calmly walked over to the table by the armchair to pick up her cigarette. Turning back to Starkwedder, she said, 'Oh yes, you are! You'll have to! You can't back out now! You've told your story to the police. You can't change it.'

'What?' Starkwedder gasped, taken aback.

Laura sat in the armchair. 'Whatever you know, or think you know,' she pointed out to him, 'you've got to stick to your story. You're an accessory after the fact — you said so yourself.' She drew on her cigarette.

Starkwedder rose and faced her. Dumbfounded, he exclaimed, 'Well, I'm damned! You little bitch!' He glared at her for a few moments without saying anything further, then suddenly turned on his heel, went swiftly to the french windows, and left. Laura watched him striding across the garden. She made a movement as though to follow and call him back, but then apparently thought better of it. With a troubled look on her face, she slowly turned away from the windows.

12

Later that day, towards the end of the afternoon, Julian Farrar paced nervously up and down in the study. The french windows to the terrace were open, and the sun was about to set, throwing a golden light onto the lawn outside. Farrar had been summoned by Laura Warwick, who apparently needed to see him urgently. He kept glancing at his watch as he awaited her.

Farrar seemed very upset and distraught. He looked out onto the terrace, turned back into the room again, and glanced at his watch. Then, noticing a newspaper on the table by the armchair, he picked it up. It was a local paper, *The Western Echo*, with a news story on the front page reporting Richard Warwick's death. 'PROMINENT LOCAL RESIDENT MURDERED BY MYSTERIOUS ASSAILANT,' the headline announced. Farrar sat in the armchair and began nervously to read the report. After a moment, he flung the paper aside, and strode over to the french windows. With a final glance back into the room, he set off across the lawn. He was halfway across the garden, when he heard a sound behind him.

Turning, he called, 'Laura, I'm sorry I — ' and then stopped, disappointed, as he saw that the person coming towards him was not Laura Warwick, but Angell, the late Richard Warwick's valet and attendant.

'Mrs Warwick asked me to say she will be down in a moment, sir,' said Angell as he approached Farrar. 'But I wondered if I might have a brief word with you?'

'Yes, yes. What is it?'

Angell came up to Julian Farrar, and walked on for a pace or two further away from the house, as if anxious that their talk should not be overheard. 'Well?' said Farrar, following him.

'I am rather worried, sir,' Angell began, 'about my own position in the house, and I felt I would like to consult you on the matter.'

His mind full of his own affairs, Julian Farrar was not really interested. 'Well, what's the trouble?' he asked.

Angell thought for a moment before replying. Then, 'Mr Warwick's death, sir,' he said, 'it puts me out of a job.'

'Yes. Yes, I suppose it does,' Farrar responded. 'But I imagine you will easily get another, won't you?'

'I hope so, sir,' Angell replied.

'You're a qualified man, aren't you?' Farrar asked him.

'Oh, yes, sir. I'm qualified,' Angell replied, 'and there is always either hospital work or private work to be obtained. I know that.'

'Then what's troubling you?'

'Well, sir,' Angell told him, 'the circumstances in which this job came to an end are very distasteful to me.'

'In plain English,' Farrar remarked, 'you don't like having been mixed up with murder. Is that it?'

'You could put it that way, sir,' the valet confirmed.

'Well,' said Farrar, 'I'm afraid there is nothing anyone can do about that. Presumably you'll get a satisfactory reference from Mrs Warwick.' He took out his cigarette-case and opened it.

'I don't think there will be any difficulty about that, sir,' Angell responded. 'Mrs Warwick is a very nice lady — a very charming lady, if I may say so.' There was a faint insinuation in his tone.

Julian Farrar, having decided to await Laura after all, was about to go back into the house. However, he turned, struck by something in the valet's manner. 'What do you mean?' he asked quietly.

'I shouldn't like to inconvenience Mrs Warwick in any way,' Angell replied, unctuously.

Before speaking, Farrar took a cigarette from his case, and then returned the case to his pocket. 'You mean,' he said, 'you're — stopping on a bit to oblige her?'

'That is quite true, sir,' Angell affirmed. 'I am helping out in the house. But that is not exactly what I meant.' He paused, and then continued, 'It's a matter, really — of my conscience, sir.'

'What in hell do you mean — your conscience?' Farrar asked sharply.

Angell looked uncomfortable, but his voice was quite confident as he continued, 'I don't think you quite appreciate my difficulties, sir. In the matter of giving my evidence to the police, that is. It is my duty as a citizen to assist the police in any manner possible. At the same time, I wish to remain loyal to my employers.'

Julian Farrar turned away to light his cigarette. 'You speak as though there was a conflict,' he said quietly.

'If you think about it, sir,' Angell remarked, 'you will realize that there is bound to be a conflict — a conflict of loyalties if I may so put it.'

Farrar looked directly at the valet. 'Just exactly what are you getting at, Angell?' he asked.

'The police, sir, are not in a position to

appreciate the background,' Angell replied. 'The background might — I just say *might* — be very important in a case like this. Also, of late I have been suffering rather severely from insomnia.'

'Do your ailments have to come into this?' Farrar asked him sharply.

'Unfortunately they do, sir,' was the valet's smooth reply. 'I retired early last night, but I was unable to get to sleep.'

'I'm sorry about that,' Farrar commiserated drily, 'but really — '

'You see, sir,' Angell continued, ignoring the interruption, 'owing to the position of my bedroom in this house, I have become aware of certain matters of which perhaps the police are not fully cognizant.'

'Just what are you trying to say?' Farrar asked, coldly.

'The late Mr Warwick, sir,' Angell replied, 'was a sick man and a cripple. It's really only to be expected under those sad circumstances that an attractive lady like Mrs Warwick might — how shall I put it? — form an attachment elsewhere.'

'So that's it, is it?' said Farrar. 'I don't think I like your tone, Angell.'

'No, sir,' Angell murmured. 'But please don't be too precipitate in your judgement. Just think it over, sir. You will perhaps realize my difficulty. Here I am, in possession of knowledge which I have not, so far, communicated to the police — but knowledge which, perhaps, it is my duty to communicate to them.'

Julian Farrar stared at Angell coldly. 'I think,' he said, 'that this story of going to the police with your information is all ballyhoo. What you're really doing is suggesting that you're in a position to stir up dirt unless — ' he paused, and then completed his sentence: ' — unless what?'

Angell shrugged his shoulders. 'I am, of course, as you have just pointed out,' he observed, 'a fully qualified nurse-attendant. But there are times, Major Farrar, when I feel I would like to set up on my own. A small — not a nursing-home, exactly — but an establishment where I could take on perhaps five or six patients. With an assistant, of course. The patients would probably include gentlemen who are alcoholically difficult to manage at home. That sort of thing. Unfortunately, although I have accumulated a certain amount of savings, they are not enough. I wondered — ' His voice trailed off suggestively.

Julian Farrar completed his thought for him. 'You wondered,' he said, 'if I — or I and Mrs Warwick together — could come to your assistance in this project, no doubt.'

'I just wondered, sir,' Angell replied meekly. 'It would be a great kindness on your part.'

'Yes, it would, wouldn't it?' Farrar observed sarcastically.

'You suggested rather harshly,' Angell went on, 'that I'm threatening to stir up dirt. Meaning, I take it, scandal. But it's not that at all, sir. I wouldn't dream of doing such a thing.'

'What exactly is it you are driving at, Angell?' Farrar sounded as though he were beginning to lose his patience. 'You're certainly driving at something.'

Angell gave a self-deprecating smile before replying. Then he spoke quietly but with emphasis. 'As I say, sir, last night I couldn't sleep very well. I was lying awake, listening to the booming of the foghorn. An extremely depressing sound I always find it, sir. Then it seemed to me that I heard a shutter banging. A very irritating noise when you're trying to get to sleep. I got up and leaned out of my window. It seemed to be the shutter of the pantry window, almost immediately below me.'

'Well?' asked Farrar, sharply.

'I decided, sir, to go down and attend to the shutter,' Angell continued. 'As I was on my way downstairs, I heard a shot.' He paused briefly. 'I didn't think anything of it at the time. 'Mr Warwick at it again,' I thought. 'But surely he can't see what he's shooting at in a mist like this.' I went to the pantry, sir, and fastened back the shutter securely. But, as I was standing there, feeling a bit uneasy for some reason, I heard footsteps coming along the path outside the window — '

'You mean,' Farrar interrupted, 'the path that — ' His eyes went towards it.

'Yes, sir,' Angell agreed. 'The path that leads from the terrace, around the corner of the house, that way — past the domestic offices. A path that's not used very much, except of course by you, sir, when you come over here, seeing as it's a short cut from your house to this one.'

He stopped speaking, and looked intently at Julian Farrar, who merely said icily, 'Go on.'

'I was feeling, as I said, a bit uneasy,' Angell continued, 'thinking there might be a prowler about. I can't tell you how relieved I was, sir, to see *you* pass the pantry window, walking quickly — hurrying on your way back home.'

After a pause, Farrar said, 'I can't really see any point in what you're telling me. Is there supposed to be one?'

With an apologetic cough, Angell answered

him. 'I just wondered, sir, whether you have mentioned to the police that you came over here last night to see Mr Warwick. In case you have not done so, and supposing that they should question me further as to the events of last night — '

Farrar interrupted him. 'You do realize, don't you,' he asked tersely, 'that the penalty for blackmail is severe?'

'Blackmail, sir?' responded Angell, sounding shocked. 'I don't know what you mean. It's just a question, as I said, of deciding where my duty lies. The police — '

'The police,' Farrar interrupted him sharply, 'are perfectly satisfied as to who killed Mr Warwick. The fellow practically signed his name to the crime. They're not likely to come asking you any more questions.'

'I assure you, sir,' Angell interjected, with alarm in his voice, 'I only meant — '

'You know perfectly well,' Farrar interrupted again, 'that you couldn't have recognized anybody in that thick fog last night. You've simply invented this story in order to — ' He broke off, as he saw Laura Warwick emerging from the house into the garden.

13

'I'm sorry I've kept you waiting, Julian,' Laura called as she approached them. She looked surprised to see Angell and Julian Farrar apparently in conversation.

'Perhaps I may speak to you later, sir, about this little matter,' the valet murmured to Farrar. He moved away, half bowing to Laura, then walked quickly across the garden and around a corner of the house.

Laura watched him go, and then spoke urgently. 'Julian,' she said, 'I must — '

Farrar interrupted her. 'Why did you send for me, Laura?' he asked, sounding annoyed.

'I've been expecting you all day,' Laura replied, surprised.

'Well, I've been up to my ears ever since this morning,' Farrar exclaimed. 'Committees, and more meetings this afternoon. I can't just drop any of these things so soon before the election. And in any case, don't you see, Laura, that it's much better that we shouldn't meet at present?'

'But there are things we've got to discuss,' Laura told him.

Taking her arm briefly, Farrar led her

further away from the house. 'Do you know that Angell is setting out to blackmail me?' he asked her.

'Angell?' cried Laura, incredulously. 'Angell is?'

'Yes. He obviously knows about us — and he also knows, or at any rate pretends to know, that I was here last night.'

Laura gasped. 'Do you mean he saw you?'

'He *says* he saw me,' Farrar retorted.

'But he couldn't have seen you in that fog,' Laura insisted.

'He's got some story,' Farrar told her, 'about coming down to the pantry and doing something to the shutter outside the window, and seeing me pass on my way home. He also says he heard a shot, not long before that, but didn't think anything of it.'

'Oh my God!' Laura gasped. 'How awful! What are we going to do?'

Farrar made an involuntary gesture as though he were about to comfort Laura with an embrace, but then, glancing towards the house, thought better of it. He gazed at her steadily. 'I don't know yet what we're going to do,' he told her. 'We'll have to think.'

'You're not going to pay him, surely?'

'No, no,' Farrar assured her. 'If one starts doing that, it's the beginning of the end. And yet, what is one to do?' He passed a hand across his brow. 'I didn't think anyone knew I came over yesterday evening,' he continued. 'I'm certain my housekeeper didn't. The point is, did Angell really see me, or is he pretending he did?'

'Supposing he does go to the police?' Laura asked, tremulously.

'I know,' murmured Farrar. Again, he ran his hand across his brow. 'One's got to think — think carefully.' He began to walk to and fro. 'Either bluff it out — say he's lying, that I never left home yesterday evening — '

'But there are the fingerprints,' Laura told him.

'What fingerprints?' asked Farrar, startled.

'You've forgotten,' Laura reminded him. 'The fingerprints on the table. The police have been thinking that they're MacGregor's, but if Angell goes to them with this story, then they'll ask to take your fingerprints, and then — '

She broke off. Julian Farrar now looked very worried. 'Yes, yes, I see,' he muttered. 'All right, then. I'll have to admit that I came over here and — tell some story. I came over to see Richard about something, and we talked — '

'You can say he was perfectly all right when you left him,' Laura suggested, speaking quickly.

There was little trace of affection in Farrar's eyes as he looked at her. 'How easy you make it sound!' he retorted, hotly. 'Can I really say that?' he added sarcastically.

'One has to say something!' she told him, sounding defensive.

'Yes, I must have put my hand there as I bent over to see — ' He swallowed, as the scene came back to him.

'So long as they believe the prints are MacGregor's,' said Laura, eagerly.

'MacGregor! MacGregor!' Farrar exclaimed angrily. He was almost shouting now. 'What on earth made you think of cooking up that message from the newspaper and putting it on Richard's body? Weren't you taking a terrific chance?'

'Yes — no — I don't know,' Laura cried in confusion.

Farrar looked at her with silent revulsion. 'So damned cold-blooded,' he muttered.

'We had to think of something,' Laura sighed. 'I — I just couldn't think. It was really Michael's idea.'

'Michael?'

'Michael — Starkwedder,' Laura told him.

'You mean he helped you?' Farrar asked. He sounded incredulous.

'Yes, yes, yes!' Laura cried impatiently. 'That's why I wanted to see you — to explain to you — '

Farrar came up close to her. His tone was

icily jealous as he asked, firmly, 'What's *Michael*' — he emphasized Starkwedder's Christian name with a cold anger — 'what's Michael Starkwedder doing in all this?'

'He came in and — and found me there,' Laura told him. 'I'd — I'd got the gun in my hand and — '

'Good God!' Farrar exclaimed with distaste, moving away from her. 'And somehow you persuaded him — '

'I think he persuaded me,' Laura murmured sadly. She moved closer to him. 'Oh, Julian — ' she began.

Her arms were about to go around his neck, but he pushed her away slightly. 'I've told you, I'll do anything I can,' he assured her. 'Don't think I won't — but — '

Laura looked at him steadily. 'You've changed,' she said quietly.

'I'm sorry, but I can't feel the same,' Farrar admitted desperately. 'After what's happened — I just can't feel the same.'

'I can,' Laura assured him. 'At least, I think I can. No matter what you'd done, Julian, I'd always feel the same.'

'Never mind our feelings for the moment,' said Farrar. 'We've got to get down to facts.'

Laura looked at him. 'I know,' she said. 'I — I told Starkwedder that I'd — you know, that I'd done it.'

Farrar looked at her incredulously. 'You told Starkwedder that?'

'Yes.'

'And he agreed to help you? He — a stranger? The man must be mad!'

Stung, Laura retorted, 'I think perhaps he *is* a little mad. But he was very comforting.'

'So! No man can resist you,' Farrar exclaimed angrily. 'Is that it?' He took a step away from her, and then turned to face her again. 'All the same, Laura, murder — ' His voice died away and he shook his head.

'I shall try never to think of it,' Laura answered. 'And it wasn't premeditated, Julian. It *was* just an impulse.' She spoke almost pleadingly.

'There's no need to go back over it all,' Farrar told her. 'We've got to think now what we're going to do.'

'I know,' she replied. 'There are the fingerprints and your lighter.'

'Yes,' he recalled. 'I must have dropped it as I leaned over his body.'

'Starkwedder knows it's yours,' Laura told him. 'But he can't do anything about it. He's committed himself. He can't change his story now.'

Julian Farrar looked at her for a moment. When he spoke, his voice had a slightly heroic tone. 'If it comes to it, Laura, I'll take the blame,' he assured her.

'No, I don't want you to,' Laura cried. She clasped his arm, and then released him quickly with a nervous glance towards the house. 'I don't want you to!' she repeated urgently.

'You mustn't think that I don't understand — how it happened,' said Farrar, speaking with an effort. 'You picked up the gun, shot him without really knowing what you were doing, and — '

Laura gave a gasp of surprise. 'What? Are you trying to make me say *I* killed him?' she cried.

'Not at all,' Farrar responded. He sounded embarrassed. 'I've told you I'm perfectly prepared to take the blame if it comes to it.'

Laura shook her head in confusion. 'But — you said — ' she began. 'You said you knew how it happened.'

He looked at her steadily. 'Listen, Laura,' he said. 'I don't think you did it deliberately. I don't think it was premeditated. I know it wasn't. I know quite well that you only shot him because — '

Laura interrupted quickly. '*I* shot him?' she gasped. 'Are you really pretending to believe that *I* shot him?'

Turning his back on her, Farrar exclamed angrily, 'For God's sake, this is impossible if

124

we're not going to be honest with each other!'

Laura sounded desperate as, trying not to shout, she announced clearly and emphatically, 'I didn't shoot him, and you know it!'

There was a pause. Julian Farrar slowly turned to face her. 'Then who did?' he asked. Suddenly realizing, he added, 'Laura! Are you trying to say that *I* shot him?'

They stood facing each other, neither of them speaking for a moment. Then Laura said, 'I heard the shot, Julian.' She took a deep breath before continuing. 'I heard the shot, and your footsteps on the path going away. I came down, and there he was — dead.'

After a pause Farrar said quietly, 'Laura, I didn't shoot him.' He gazed up at the sky as though seeking help or inspiration, and then looked at her intently. 'I came over here to see Richard,' he explained, 'to tell him that after the election we'd got to come to some arrangement about a divorce. I heard a shot just before I got here. I just thought it was Richard up to his tricks as usual. I came in here, and there he was. Dead. He was still warm.'

Laura was now very perplexed. 'Warm?' she echoed.

'He hadn't been dead more than a minute or two,' said Farrar. 'Of course I believed you'd shot him. Who else could have shot him?'

'I don't understand,' Laura murmured.

'I suppose — I suppose it could have been suicide,' Farrar began, but Laura interrupted him. 'No, it couldn't, because — '

She broke off, as they both heard Jan's voice inside the house, shouting excitedly.

14

Julian Farrar and Laura ran towards the house, almost colliding with Jan as he emerged through the french windows. 'Laura,' Jan cried as she gently but firmly propelled him back into the study. 'Laura, now that Richard's dead, all of his pistols and guns and things belong to me, don't they? I mean, I'm his brother, I'm the next man in the family.'

Julian Farrar followed them into the room and wandered distractedly across to the armchair, sitting on an arm of it as Laura attempted to pacify Jan who was now complaining petulantly, 'Benny won't let me have his guns. She's locked them up in the cupboard in there.' He waved vaguely towards the door. 'But they're mine. I've got a right to them. Make her give me the key.'

'Now listen, Jan darling,' Laura began, but Jan would not be interrupted. He went quickly to the door, and then turned back to her, exclaiming, 'She treats me like a child. Benny, I mean. Everyone treats me like a child. But I'm not a child, I'm a man. I'm nineteen. I'm nearly of age.' He stretched his arms across the door as though protecting his guns. 'All of

Richard's sporting things belong to me. I'm going to do what Richard did. I'm going to shoot squirrels and birds and cats.' He laughed hysterically. 'I might shoot people, too, if I don't like them.'

'You mustn't get too excited, Jan,' Laura warned him.

'I'm not excited,' Jan cried petulantly. 'But I'm not going to be — what's it called? — I'm not going to be victimized.' He came back into the centre of the room, and faced Laura squarely. 'I'm master here now. I'm the master of this house. Everybody's got to do as I say.' He paused, then turned and addressed Julian Farrar. 'I could be a JP if I wanted to, couldn't I, Julian?'

'I think you're a little young for that yet,' Farrar told him.

Jan shrugged, and turned back to Laura. 'You all treat me like a child,' he complained again. 'But you can't do it any longer — not now that Richard's dead.' He flung himself onto the sofa, legs sprawling. 'I expect I'm rich, too, aren't I?' he added. 'This house belongs to me. Nobody can push me around any longer. I can push *them* around. I'm not going to be dictated to by silly old Benny. If Benny tries ordering me about, I shall — ' He paused, then added childishly, 'I know what I shall do!'

Laura approached him. 'Listen, Jan darling,' she murmured gently. 'It's a very worrying time for all of us, and Richard's things don't belong to anybody until the lawyers have come and read his will and granted what they call probate. That's what happens when anyone dies. Until then, we all have to wait and see. Do you understand?'

Laura's tone had a calming and quietening effect on Jan. He looked up at her, then put his arms around her waist, nestling close to her. 'I understand what you tell me, Laura,' he said. 'I love you, Laura. I love you very much.'

'Yes, darling,' Laura murmured soothingly. 'I love you, too.'

'You're glad Richard's dead, aren't you?' Jan asked her suddenly.

Slightly startled, Laura replied hurriedly, 'No, of course I'm not glad.'

'Oh yes, you are,' said Jan, slyly. 'Now you can marry Julian.'

Laura looked quickly at Julian Farrar, who rose to his feet as Jan continued, 'You've wanted to marry Julian for a long time, haven't you? *I* know. They think I don't notice or know things. But I do. And so it's all right for both of you now. It's been made all right for you, and you're both pleased. You're pleased, because — '

He broke off, hearing Miss Bennett out in

129

the corridor calling, 'Jan!', and laughed. 'Silly old Benny!' he shouted, bouncing up and down on the sofa.

'Now, do be nice to Benny,' Laura cautioned Jan, as she pulled him to his feet. 'She's having such a lot of trouble and worry over all this.' Guiding Jan to the door, Laura continued gently, 'You must help Benny, Jan, because you're the man of the family now.'

Jan opened the door, then looked from Laura to Julian. 'All right, all right,' he promised, with a smile. 'I will.' He left the room, shutting the door behind him and calling 'Benny!' as he went.

Laura turned to Julian Farrar who had risen from his armchair and walked over to her. 'I'd no idea he knew about us,' she exclaimed.

'That's the trouble with people like Jan,' Farrar retorted. 'You never know how much or how little they do know. He's very — well, he gets rather easily out of hand, doesn't he?'

'Yes, he does get easily excited,' Laura admitted. 'But now that Richard isn't here to tease him, he'll calm down. He'll get to be more normal. I'm sure he will.'

Julian Farrar looked doubtful. 'Well, I don't know about that,' he began, but broke off as Starkwedder suddenly appeared at the french windows.

'Hello — good evening,' Starkwedder called, sounding quite happy.

'Oh — er — good evening,' Farrar replied, hesitantly.

'How's everything? Bright and cheerful?' Starkwedder enquired, looking from one to the other. He suddenly grinned. 'I see,' he observed. 'Two's company and three's none.' He stepped into the room. 'Shouldn't have come in by the window this way. A gentleman would have gone to the front door and rung the bell. Is that it? But then, you see, I'm no gentleman.'

'Oh, please — ' Laura began, but Starkwedder interrupted her. 'As a matter of fact,' he explained, 'I've come for two reasons. First, to say goodbye. My character's been cleared. High-level cables from Abadan saying what a fine, upright fellow I am. So I'm free to depart.'

'I'm so sorry you're going — so soon,' Laura told him, with genuine feeling in her voice.

'That's nice of you,' Starkwedder responded with a touch of bitterness, 'considering the way I butted in on your family murder.' He looked at her for a moment, then moved across to the desk chair. 'But I came in by the window for another reason,' he went on. 'The police brought me up in their car. And, although they're being very tight-lipped about it, it's my belief there's something up!'

Dismayed, Laura gasped, 'The police have come back?'

'Yes,' Starkwedder affirmed, decisively.

'But I thought they'd finished this morning,' said Laura.

Starkwedder gave her a shrewd look. 'That's why I say — something's up!' he exclaimed.

There were voices in the corridor outside. Laura and Julian Farrar drew together as the door opened, and Richard Warwick's mother came in, looking very upright and self-possessed, though still walking with the aid of a cane.

'Benny!' Mrs Warwick called over her shoulder, and then addressed Laura. 'Oh, there you are, Laura. We've been looking for you.'

Julian Farrar went to Mrs Warwick and helped her into the armchair. 'How kind you are to come over again, Julian,' the old lady exclaimed, 'when we all know how busy you are.'

'I would have come before, Mrs Warwick,' Farrar told her, as he settled her in the chair, 'but it's been a particularly hectic day. Anything that I can possibly do to help — ' He stopped speaking as Miss Bennett entered followed by Inspector Thomas. Carrying a briefcase, the inspector moved to take up a central position. Starkwedder went to sit in the desk chair, and lit a cigarette as Sergeant Cadwallader came in with Angell, who closed the door and stood with his back to it.

'I can't find young Mr Warwick, sir,' the sergeant reported, crossing to the french windows.

'He's out somewhere. Gone for a walk,' Miss Bennett announced.

'It doesn't matter,' said the inspector. There was a momentary pause as he surveyed the occupants of the room. His manner had changed, for it now had a grimness it did not have before.

After waiting a moment for him to speak, Mrs Warwick asked coldly, 'Do I understand that you have further questions to ask us, Inspector Thomas?'

'Yes, Mrs Warwick,' he replied, 'I'm afraid I have.'

Mrs Warwick's voice sounded weary as she asked, 'You still have no news of this man MacGregor?'

'On the contrary.'

'He's been found?' Mrs Warwick asked, eagerly.

'Yes,' was the inspector's terse reply.

There was a definite reaction of excitement

133

from the assembled company. Laura and Julian Farrar looked incredulous, and Starkwedder turned in his chair to face the inspector.

Miss Bennett's voice suddenly rang out sharply. 'You've arrested him, then?'

The inspector looked at her for a moment before replying. Then, 'That, I'm afraid, would be impossible, Miss Bennett,' he informed her.

'Impossible?' Mrs Warwick interjected. 'But why?'

'Because he's dead,' the inspector replied, quietly.

15

A shocked silence greeted Inspector Thomas's announcement. Then, hesitantly and, it seemed, fearfully, Laura whispered, 'Wh- what did you say?'

'I said that this man MacGregor is dead,' the inspector affirmed.

There were gasps from everyone in the room, and the inspector expanded upon his terse announcement. 'John MacGregor,' he told them, 'died in Alaska over two years ago — not very long after he returned to Canada from England.'

'Dead!' Laura exclaimed, incredulously.

Unnoticed by anyone in the room, young Jan passed quickly along the terrace outside the french windows, and disappeared from view.

'That makes a difference, doesn't it?' the inspector continued. 'It wasn't John MacGregor who put that revenge note on the dead body of Mr Warwick. But it's clear, isn't it, that it was put there by someone who knew all about MacGregor and the accident in Norfolk. Which ties it in, very definitely, with someone in this house.'

'No,' Miss Bennett exclaimed sharply. 'No, it could have been — surely it could have been — ' She broke off.

'Yes, Miss Bennett?' the inspector prompted her. He waited for a moment, but Miss Bennett could not continue. Suddenly looking completely broken, she moved away towards the french windows.

The inspector turned his attention to Richard Warwick's mother. 'You'll understand, madam,' he said, attempting to put a note of sympathy into his voice, 'that this alters things.'

'Yes, I see that,' Mrs Warwick replied. She rose. 'Do you need me any further, Inspector?' she asked.

'Not for the moment, Mrs Warwick,' the inspector told her.

'Thank you,' Mrs Warwick murmured as she went to the door, which Angell hastened to open for her. Julian Farrar helped the old lady to the door. As she left the room, he returned and stood behind the armchair, looking pensive. Meanwhile, Inspector Thomas had been opening his briefcase, and was now taking out a gun.

Angell was about to follow Mrs Warwick from the room when the inspector called, peremptorily, 'Angell!'

The valet gave a start, and turned back into

136

the room, closing the door. 'Yes, sir?' he responded quietly.

The inspector approached him, carrying what was clearly the murder weapon. 'About this gun,' he asked the valet. 'You were uncertain this morning. Can you, or can you not, say definitely that it belonged to Mr Warwick?'

'I wouldn't like to be definite, Inspector,' Angell replied. 'He had so many, you see.'

'This one is a continental weapon,' the inspector informed him, holding the gun out in front of him. 'It's a war souvenir of some kind, I'd say.'

As he was speaking, again apparently unnoticed by anyone in the room Jan passed along the terrace outside, going in the opposite direction, and carrying a gun which he seemed to be attempting to conceal.

Angell looked at the weapon. 'Mr Warwick did have some foreign guns, sir,' he stated. 'But he looked after all his shooting equipment himself. He wouldn't let me touch them.'

The inspector went over to Julian Farrar. 'Major Farrar,' he said, 'you probably have war souvenirs. Does this weapon mean anything to you?'

Farrar glanced at the gun casually. 'Not a thing, I'm afraid,' he answered.

Turning away from him, the inspector went to replace the gun in his briefcase. 'Sergeant

Cadwallader and I,' he announced, turning to face the assembled company, 'will want to go over Mr Warwick's collection of weapons very carefully. He had permits for most of them, I understand.'

'Oh yes, sir,' Angell assured him. 'The permits are in one of the drawers in his bedroom. And all the guns and other weapons are in the gun cupboard.'

Sergeant Cadwallader went to the door, but was stopped by Miss Bennett before he could leave the room. 'Wait a minute,' she called to him. 'You'll want the key of the gun cupboard.' She took a key from her pocket.

'You locked it up?' the inspector queried, turning sharply to her. 'Why was that?'

Miss Bennett's retort was equally sharp. 'I should hardly think you'd need to ask that,' she snapped. 'All those guns, and ammunition as well. Highly dangerous. Everyone knows that.'

Concealing a grin, the sergeant took the key she offered him, and went to the door, pausing in the doorway to see whether the inspector wished to accompany him. Sounding distinctly annoyed at Miss Bennett's uncalled-for comment, Inspector Thomas remarked, 'I shall need to talk to you again, Angell,' as he picked up his briefcase and left the room. The sergeant followed him, leaving the door open for Angell.

However, the valet did not leave the room immediately. Instead, after a nervous glance at Laura who now sat staring at the floor, he went up to Julian Farrar, and murmured, 'About that little matter, sir. I am anxious to get something settled soon. If you could see your way, sir — '

Speaking with difficulty, Farrar answered, 'I think — something — could be managed.'

'Thank you, sir,' Angell responded with a faint smile on his face. 'Thank you very much, sir.' He went to the door and was about to leave the room when Farrar stopped him with a peremptory 'No! Wait a moment, Angell.'

As the valet turned to face him, Farrar called loudly, 'Inspector Thomas!'

There was a tense pause. Then, after a moment or two, the inspector appeared in the doorway, with the sergeant behind him. 'Yes, Major Farrar?' the inspector asked, quietly.

Resuming a pleasant, natural manner, Julian Farrar strolled across to the armchair. 'Before you get busy with routine, Inspector,' he remarked, 'there is something I ought to have told you. Really, I suppose, I should have mentioned it this morning. But we were all so upset. Mrs Warwick has just informed me that there are some fingerprints that you are anxious to identify. On the table here, I think you said.' He paused, then added, easily, 'In all probability, Inspector, those are my fingerprints.'

There was a pause. The inspector slowly approached Farrar, and then asked quietly, but with an accusing note in his voice, 'You were over here last night, Major Farrar?'

'Yes,' Farrar replied. 'I came over, as I often do after dinner, to have a chat with Richard.'

'And you found him — ?' the inspector prompted.

'I found him very moody and depressed. So I didn't stay long.'

'At about what time was this, Major Farrar?'

Farrar thought for a moment, and then replied, 'I really can't remember. Perhaps ten o'clock, or ten-thirty. Thereabouts.'

The inspector regarded him steadily. 'Can you get a little closer than that?' he asked.

'I'm sorry. I'm afraid I can't,' was Farrar's immediate answer.

After a somewhat tense pause, the inspector asked, trying to sound casual, 'I don't suppose there would have been any quarrel — or bad words of any kind?'

'No, certainly not,' Farrar retorted indignantly. He looked at his watch. 'I'm late,' he observed. 'I've got to take the chair at a meeting in the Town Hall. I can't keep them waiting.' He turned and walked towards the french windows. 'So, if you don't mind — ' He paused on the terrace.

'Mustn't keep the Town Hall waiting,' the inspector agreed, following him. 'But I'm sure you'll understand, Major Farrar, that I should like a full statement from you of your movements last night. Perhaps we could do this tomorrow morning.' He paused, and then continued, 'You realize, of course, that there is no obligation on you to make a statement, that it is purely voluntary on your part — and that you are fully entitled to have your solicitor present, should you so wish.'

Mrs Warwick had re-entered the room. She stood in the doorway, leaving the door open, and listening to the inspector's last few words. Julian Farrar drew in his breath as he grasped the significance of what the inspector had said. 'I understand — perfectly,' he said. 'Shall we say ten o'clock tomorrow morning? And my solicitor will be present'

Farrar made his exit along the terrace, and the inspector turned to Laura Warwick. 'Did you see Major Farrar when he came here last night?' he asked her.

'I — I — ,' Laura began uncertainly, but was interrupted by Starkwedder who suddenly jumped up from his chair and went across to them, interposing himself between the inspector and Laura. 'I don't think Mrs Warwick feels like answering any questions just now,' he said.

16

Starkwedder and Inspector Thomas faced each other in silence for a moment. Then the inspector spoke. 'What did you say, Mr Starkwedder?' he asked, quietly.

'I said,' Starkwedder replied, 'that I don't think Mrs Warwick feels like any more questions just at the moment.'

'Indeed?' growled the inspector. 'And what business is it of yours, might I ask?'

Mrs Warwick senior joined in the confrontation. 'Mr Starkwedder is quite right,' she announced.

The inspector turned to Laura questioningly. After a pause, she murmured, 'No, I don't want to answer any more questions just now.'

Looking rather smug, Starkwedder smiled at the inspector who turned away angrily and swiftly left the room with the sergeant. Angell followed them, shutting the door behind him. As he did so, Laura burst out, 'But I should speak. I must — I must tell them — '

'Mr Starkwedder is quite right, Laura,' Mrs Warwick interjected forcefully. 'The less you say now, the better.' She took a few paces about the room, leaning heavily on her stick, and then continued. 'We must get in touch with Mr Adams at once.' Turning to Starkwedder, she explained, 'Mr Adams is our solicitor.' She glanced across at Miss Bennett. 'Ring him up now, Benny.'

Miss Bennett nodded and went towards the telephone, but Mrs Warwick stopped her. 'No, use the extension upstairs,' she instructed, adding, 'Laura, go with her.'

Laura rose, and then hesitated, looking confusedly at her mother-in-law, who merely added, 'I want to talk to Mr Starkwedder.'

'But — ' Laura began, only to be immediately interrupted by Mrs Warwick. 'Now don't worry, my dear,' the old lady assured her. 'Just do as I say.'

Laura hesitated for a moment, then went out into the hall, followed by Miss Bennett who closed the door. Mrs Warwick immediately went up to Starkwedder. 'I don't know how much time we have,' she said, speaking rapidly and glancing towards the door. 'I want you to help me.'

Starkwedder looked surprised. 'How?' he asked.

After a pause, Mrs Warwick spoke again. 'You're an intelligent man — and you're a stranger. You've come into our lives from outside. We know nothing about you. You've nothing to do with any of us.'

Starkwedder nodded. 'The unexpected guest, eh?' he murmured. He perched on an arm of the sofa. 'That's been said to me already,' he remarked.

'Because you're a stranger,' Mrs Warwick continued, 'there is something I'm going to ask you to do for me.' She moved across to the french windows and stepped out onto the terrace, looking along it in both directions.

After a pause, Starkwedder spoke. 'Yes, Mrs Warwick?'

Coming back into the room, Mrs Warwick began to speak with some urgency. 'Up until this evening,' she told him, 'there was a reasonable explanation for this tragedy. A man whom my son had injured — by accidentally killing his child — came to take his revenge. I know it sounds melodramatic, but, after all, one does read of such things happening.'

'As you say,' Starkwedder remarked, wondering where this conversation was leading.

'But now, I'm afraid that explanation has gone,' Mrs Warwick continued. 'And it brings the murder of my son back into the family.' She took a few steps towards the armchair. 'Now, there are two people who definitely could not have shot my son. And they are his wife and Miss Bennett. They were actually together when the shot was fired.'

Starkwedder gave a quick look at her, but all he said was, 'Quite.'

'However,' Mrs Warwick continued, 'although Laura could not have shot her husband, she could have known who did.'

'That would make her an accessory before the fact,' Starkwedder remarked. 'She and this Julian Farrar chap in it together? Is that what you mean?'

A look of annoyance crossed Mrs Warwick's face. 'That is *not* what I mean,' she told him. She cast another quick glance at the door, and then continued, 'Julian Farrar did not shoot my son.'

Starkwedder rose from the arm of the sofa. 'How can you possibly know that?' he asked her.

'I do know it,' was Mrs Warwick's reply. She looked steadily at him. 'I am going to tell you, a stranger, something that none of my family know,' she stated calmly. 'It is this. I am a woman who has not very long to live.'

'I am sorry — ' Starkwedder began, but Mrs Warwick raised her hand to stop him. 'I am not telling you this for sympathy,' she remarked. 'I am telling you in order to explain what otherwise might be difficult of explanation. There are times when you decide on a course of action which you would not

146

decide upon if you had several years of life before you.'

'Such as?' asked Starkwedder quietly.

Mrs Warwick regarded him steadily. 'First, I must tell you something else, Mr Starkwedder,' she said. 'I must tell you something about my son.' She went to the sofa and sat. 'I loved my son very dearly. As a child, and in his young manhood, he had many fine qualities. He was successful, resourceful, brave, sunny-tempered, a delightful companion.' She paused, and seemed to be remembering. Then she continued. 'There were, I must admit, always the defects of those qualities in him. He was impatient of controls, of restraints. He had a cruel streak in him, and he had a kind of fatal arrogance. So long as he was successful, all was well. But he did not have the kind of nature that could deal with adversity, and for some time now I have watched him slowly go downhill.'

Starkwedder quietly seated himself on the stool, facing her.

'If I say that he had become a monster,' Richard Warwick's mother continued, 'it would sound exaggerated. And yet, in some ways he *was* a monster — a monster of egoism, of pride, of cruelty. Because he had been hurt himself, he had an enormous desire to hurt others.' A hard note crept into her voice. 'So others began to suffer because of him. Do you understand me?'

'I think so — yes,' Starkwedder murmured softly.

Mrs Warwick's voice became gentle again as she went on. 'Now, I am very fond of my daughter-in-law. She has spirit, she is warm-hearted, and she has a very brave power of endurance. Richard swept her off her feet, but I don't know whether she was ever really in love with him. However, I will tell you this — she did everything a wife could do to make Richard's illness and inaction bearable.'

She thought for a moment, and her voice was sad as she continued, 'But he would have none of her help. He rejected it. I think at times he hated her, and perhaps that's more natural than one might suppose. So, when I tell you that the inevitable happened, I think you will understand what I mean. Laura fell in love with another man, and he with her.'

Starkwedder regarded Mrs Warwick thoughtfully. 'Why are you telling me all this?' he asked.

'Because you are a stranger,' she replied, firmly. 'These loves and hates and tribulations mean nothing to you, so you can hear about them unmoved.'

'Possibly.'

As though she had not heard him, Mrs Warwick went on speaking. 'So there came a time,' she said, 'when it seemed that only one thing would solve all the difficulties. Richard's death.'

Starkwedder continued to study her face. 'And so,' he murmured, 'conveniently, Richard died?'

'Yes,' Mrs Warwick answered.

There was a pause. Then Starkwedder rose, moved around the stool, and went to the table to stub out his cigarette. 'Excuse me putting this bluntly, Mrs Warwick,' he said, 'but are you confessing to murder?'

17

Mrs Warwick was silent for a few moments. Then she said sharply, 'I will ask you a question, Mr Starkwedder. Can you understand that someone who has given life might also feel themselves entitled to take that life?'

Starkwedder paced around the room as he thought about this. Finally, 'Mothers have been known to kill their children, yes,' he admitted. 'But it's usually been for a sordid reason — insurance — or perhaps they have two or three children already and don't want to be bothered with another one.' Turning back suddenly to face her, he asked quickly, 'Does Richard's death benefit you financially?'

'No, it does not,' Mrs Warwick replied firmly.

Starkwedder made a deprecatory gesture. 'You must forgive my frankness — ' he began, only to be interrupted by Mrs Warwick, who asked with more than a touch of asperity in her voice, 'Do you understand what I am trying to tell you?'

'Yes, I think I do,' he replied. 'You're telling me that it's possible for a mother to kill her son.' He walked over to the sofa and leaned across it as he continued. 'And you're telling me — specifically — that it's possible that *you* killed *your* son.' He paused, and looked at her steadily. 'Is that a theory,' he asked, 'or am I to understand it as a fact?'

'I am not confessing to *anything*,' Mrs Warwick answered. 'I am merely putting before you a certain point of view. An emergency might arise at a time when I was no longer here to deal with it. And in the event of such a thing happening, I want you to have this, and to make use of it.' She took an envelope from her pocket and handed it to him.

Starkwedder took the envelope, but remarked, 'That's all very well. However, I shan't be here. I'm going back to Abadan to carry on with my job.'

Mrs Warwick made a gesture of dismissal, clearly regarding the objection as insignificant. 'You won't be out of touch with civilization,' she reminded him. 'There are newspapers, radio and so on in Abadan, presumably.'

'Oh yes,' he agreed. 'We have all the civilized blessings.'

'Then please keep that envelope. You see whom it's addressed to?'

Starkwedder glanced at the envelope. 'The Chief Constable. Yes. But I'm not at all clear what's really in your mind,' he told Mrs

Warwick. 'For a woman, you're really remarkably good at keeping a secret. Either you committed this murder yourself, or you know who did commit it. That's right, isn't it?'

She looked away from him as she replied, 'I don't propose to discuss the matter.'

Starkwedder sat in the armchair. 'And yet,' he persisted, 'I'd like very much to know exactly what is in your mind.'

'Then I'm afraid I shan't tell you,' Mrs Warwick retorted. 'As you say, I am a woman who can keep her secrets well.'

Deciding to try a different tack, Starkwedder said, 'This valet fellow — the chap who looked after your son — ' He paused as though trying to remember the valet's name.

'You mean Angell,' Mrs Warwick told him. 'Well, what about Angell?'

'Do you like him?' asked Starkwedder.

'No, I don't, as it happens,' she replied. 'But he was efficient at his job, and Richard was certainly not easy to work for.'

'I imagine not,' Starkwedder remarked. 'But Angell put up with these difficulties, did he?'

'It was made worth his while,' was Mrs Warwick's wry response.

Starkwedder again began to pace about the room. Then he turned to face Mrs Warwick

152

and, trying to draw her out, asked, 'Did Richard have anything on him?'

The old lady looked puzzled for a moment. 'On him?' she repeated. 'What do you mean? Oh, I see. You mean, did Richard know something to Angell's discredit?'

'Yes, that's what I mean,' Starkwedder affirmed. 'Did he have a hold over Angell?'

Mrs Warwick thought for a moment before replying. Then, 'No, I don't think so,' she said.

'I was just wondering — ' he began.

'You mean,' Mrs Warwick broke in, impatiently, 'did Angell shoot my son? I doubt it. I doubt that very much.'

'I see. You're not buying that one,' Starkwedder remarked. 'A pity, but there it is.'

Mrs Warwick suddenly got to her feet. 'Thank you, Mr Starkwedder,' she said. 'You have been very kind.'

She gave him her hand. Amused at her abruptness, he shook hands with her, then went to the door and opened it. After a moment she left the room. Starkwedder closed the door after her, smiling. 'Well, I'm damned!' he exclaimed to himself, as he looked again at the envelope. 'What a woman!'

Hurriedly, he put the envelope into his pocket, as Miss Bennett came into the room looking upset and preoccupied. 'What's she been saying to you?' she demanded.

Taken aback, Starkwedder played for time. 'Eh? What's that?' he responded.

'Mrs Warwick — what's she been saying?' Miss Bennett asked again.

Avoiding a direct reply, Starkwedder merely remarked, 'You seem upset.'

'Of course I'm upset,' she replied. 'I know what she's capable of.'

Starkwedder looked at the housekeeper steadily before asking, 'What *is* Mrs Warwick capable of? Murder?'

Miss Bennett took a step towards him. 'Is that what she's been trying to make you believe?' she asked. 'It isn't true, you know. You've got to realize that. It isn't true.'

'Well, one can't be sure. After all, it might be,' he observed judiciously.

'But I tell you it isn't,' she insisted.

'How can you possibly know that?' Starkwedder asked.

'I do know,' Miss Bennett replied. 'Do you think there's anything I don't know about the people in this house? I've been with them for years. Years, I tell you.' She sat in the arm-chair. 'I care for them very much, all of them.'

'Including the late Richard Warwick?' Starkwedder asked.

Miss Bennett seemed lost in thought for a

moment. Then, 'I used to be fond of him — once,' she replied.

There was a pause. Starkwedder sat on the stool and regarded her steadily before murmuring, 'Go on.'

'He changed,' said Miss Bennett. 'He became — warped. His whole mentality became quite different. Sometimes he could be a devil.'

'Yes, everybody seems to agree on that,' Starkwedder observed.

'But if you'd known him as he used to be — ' she began.

He interrupted her. 'I don't believe that, you know. I don't think people change.'

'Richard did,' Miss Bennett insisted.

'Oh, no, he didn't,' Starkwedder contradicted her. He resumed his prowling about the room. 'You've got things the wrong way round, I'll bet. I'd say he was always a devil underneath. I'd say he was one of those people who have to be happy and successful — or else! They hide their real selves as long as it gets them what they want. But underneath, the bad streak's always there.'

He turned to face Miss Bennett. 'His cruelty, I bet, was always there. He was probably a bully at school. He was attractive to women, of course. Women are always attracted by bullies. And he took a lot of his sadism out in his big-game hunting, I dare say.' He indicated the hunting trophies on the walls.

'Richard Warwick must have been a monstrous egoist,' he continued. 'That's how he seems to me from the way all you people talk about him. He enjoyed building himself up as a good fellow, generous, successful, lovable and all the rest of it.' Starkwedder was still pacing restlessly. 'But the mean streak was there, all right. And when his accident came, it was just the façade that was torn away, and you all saw him as he really was.'

Miss Bennett rose. 'I don't see that you've got any business to talk,' she exclaimed indignantly. 'You're a stranger, and you know nothing about it.'

'Perhaps not, but I've heard a great deal about it,' Starkwedder retorted. 'Everyone seems to talk to me for some reason.'

'Yes, I suppose they do. Yes, I'm talking to you now, aren't I?' she admitted, as she sat down again. 'That's because we none of us here dare talk to one another.' She looked up at him, appealingly. 'I wish you weren't going away,' she told him.

Starkwedder shook his head. 'I've done nothing to help at all, really,' he said. 'All I've done is blunder in and discover a dead body for you.'

'But it was Laura and I who discovered Richard's body,' Miss Bennett contradicted him. She paused and then suddenly added, 'Or did Laura — did you — ?' Her voice trailed off into silence.

18

Starkwedder looked at Miss Bennett and smiled. 'You're pretty sharp, aren't you?' he observed.

Miss Bennett stared at him fixedly. 'You helped her, didn't you?' she asked, making it sound like an accusation.

He walked away from her. 'Now you're imagining things,' he told her.

'Oh, no, I'm not,' Miss Bennett retorted. 'I want Laura to be happy. Oh, I so very much want her to be happy!'

Starkwedder turned to her, exclaiming passionately, 'Damn it, so do I!'

Miss Bennett looked at him in surprise. Then she began to speak. 'In that case I — I've got to — ' she began, but was interrupted. Gesturing to her to be silent, Starkwedder murmured, 'Just a minute.' He hastened to the french windows, opened a window and called, 'What are you doing?'

Miss Bennett now caught sight of Jan out on the lawn, brandishing a gun. Rising quickly, she too went across to the french windows and called urgently, 'Jan! Jan! Give me that gun.'

Jan, however, was too quick for her. He ran

off laughing, and shouting, 'Come and get it,' as he ran. Miss Bennett followed him, with urgent cries of 'Jan! Jan!'

Starkwedder looked out across the lawn, trying to see what was happening. Then he turned back, and was about to go to the door, when Laura suddenly entered the room.

'Where's the inspector?' she asked him.

Starkwedder made an ineffectual gesture. Laura shut the door behind her, and came over to him. 'Michael, you must listen to me,' she implored him. 'Julian didn't kill Richard.'

'Indeed?' Starkwedder replied coldly. 'He told you so, did he?'

'You don't believe me, but it's true.' Laura sounded desperate.

'You mean you believe it's true,' Starkwedder pointed out to her.

'No, I know it's true,' Laura replied. 'You see, he thought *I'd* killed Richard.'

Starkwedder moved back into the room, away from the french windows. 'That's not exactly surprising,' he said with an acid smile. 'I thought so, too, didn't I?'

Laura's voice sounded even more desperate as she insisted, 'He thought I'd shot Richard. But he couldn't cope with it. It made him feel — ' She stopped, embarrassed, then continued, 'It made him feel differently towards me.'

Starkwedder looked at her coldly. 'Whereas,' he pointed out, 'when you thought *he'd* killed Richard, you took it in your stride without turning a hair!' Suddenly relenting a little, he smiled. 'Women are wonderful!' he murmured. He perched on the sofa arm. 'What made Farrar come out with the damaging fact that he was here last night? Don't tell me it was a pure and simple regard for the truth?'

'It was Angell,' Laura replied. 'Angell saw — or says he saw — Julian here.'

'Yes,' Starkwedder remarked with a somewhat bitter laugh. 'I thought I got a whiff of blackmail. Not a nice fellow, Angell.'

'He says he saw Julian just after the — after the shot was fired,' Laura told him. 'Oh, I'm frightened. It's all closing in. I'm so frightened.'

Starkwedder went over to her and took her by the shoulders. 'You needn't be,' he said, reassuringly. 'It's going to be all right.'

Laura shook her head. 'It can't be,' she cried.

'It will be all right, I tell you,' he insisted, shaking her gently.

She looked at him wonderingly. 'Shall we ever know who shot Richard?' she asked him.

Starkwedder looked at her for a moment without replying, and then went to the french windows and gazed out into the garden. 'Your

Miss Bennett,' he said, 'seems very positive she knows all the answers.'

'She's always positive,' Laura replied. 'But she's sometimes wrong.'

Apparently glimpsing something outside, Starkwedder suddenly beckoned to Laura to join him. Running across to him, she took his outstretched hand. 'Yes, Laura,' he exclaimed excitedly, still looking out into the garden. 'I thought so!'

'What is it?' she asked.

'Ssh!' he cautioned. At almost the same moment, Miss Bennett came into the room from the hallway. 'Mr Starkwedder,' she said hurriedly. 'Go into the room next door — the inspector's already there. Quickly!'

Starkwedder and Laura crossed the study swiftly, and hurried into the corridor, closing the door behind them. As soon as they had gone, Miss Bennett looked out into the garden, where daylight was beginning to fade. 'Now come in, Jan,' she called to him. 'Don't tease me any more. Come in, come inside.'

19

Miss Bennett beckoned to Jan, then stepped back into the room and stood to one side of the french windows. Jan suddenly appeared from the terrace, looking half mutinous and half flushed with triumph. He was carrying a gun.

'Now, Jan, how on earth did you get hold of that?' Miss Bennett asked him.

Jan came into the room. 'Thought you were so clever, didn't you, Benny?' he said, quite belligerently. 'Very clever, locking up all Richard's guns in there.' He nodded in the direction of the hallway. 'But I found a key that fitted the gun cupboard. I've got a gun now, just like Richard. I'm going to have lots of guns and pistols. I'm going to shoot things.' He suddenly raised the gun and pointed it at Miss Bennett, who flinched. 'Be careful, Benny,' he went on with a chuckle, 'I might shoot you.'

Miss Bennett tried not to look too alarmed as she said, in as soothing a tone as she could muster, 'Why, you wouldn't do a thing like that, Jan, I know you wouldn't.'

Jan continued to point the gun at Miss

Bennett, but after a few moments he lowered it.

Miss Bennett relaxed slightly, and after a pause Jan exclaimed, sweetly and rather eagerly, 'No, I wouldn't. Of course I wouldn't.'

'After all, it's not as though you were just a careless boy,' Miss Bennett told him, reassuringly. 'You're a man now, aren't you?'

Jan beamed. He walked over to the desk and sat in the chair. 'Yes, I'm a man,' he agreed. 'Now that Richard's dead, I'm the only man in the house.'

'That's why I know you wouldn't shoot me,' Miss Bennett said. 'You'd only shoot an enemy.'

'That's right,' Jan exclaimed with delight.

Sounding as though she were choosing her words very carefully, Miss Bennett said, 'During the war, if you were in the Resistance, when you killed an enemy you put a notch on your gun.'

'Is that true?' Jan responded, examining his gun. 'Did they really?' He looked eagerly at Miss Bennett. 'Did some people have a lot of notches?'

'Yes,' she replied, 'some people had quite a lot of notches.'

Jan chortled with glee. 'What fun!' he exclaimed.

'Of course,' Miss Bennett continued, 'some

people don't like killing anything — but other people do.'

'Richard did,' Jan reminded her.

'Yes, Richard liked killing things,' Miss Bennett admitted. She turned away from him casually, as she added, 'You like killing things, too, don't you, Jan?'

Unseen by her, Jan took a penknife from his pocket and began to make a notch on his gun. 'It's exciting to kill things,' he observed, a trifle petulantly.

Miss Bennett turned back to face him. 'You didn't want Richard to have you sent away, did you, Jan?' she asked him quietly.

'He said he would,' Jan retorted with feeling. 'He was a beast!'

Miss Bennett walked around behind the desk chair in which Jan was still sitting. 'You said to Richard once,' she reminded him, 'that you'd kill him if he was going to send you away.'

'Did I?' Jan responded. He sounded nonchalantly offhand.

'But you didn't kill him?' Miss Bennett asked, her intonation making her words into only a half-question.

'Oh, no, I didn't kill him.' Again, Jan sounded unconcerned.

'That was rather weak of you,' Miss Bennett observed.

There was a crafty look in Jan's eyes as he responded, 'Was it?'

'Yes, I think so. To say you'd kill him, and then not to do it.' Miss Bennett moved around the desk, but looked towards the door. 'If anyone was threatening to shut *me* up, I'd want to kill him, and I'd do it, too.'

'Who says someone else did?' Jan retorted swiftly. 'Perhaps it *was* me.'

'Oh, no, it wouldn't be you,' Miss Bennett said, dismissively. 'You were only a boy. You wouldn't have dared.'

Jan jumped up and backed away from her. 'You think I wouldn't have dared?' His voice was almost a squeal. 'Is that what you think?'

'Of course it's what I think.' She seemed now deliberately to be taunting him. 'Of course you wouldn't have dared to kill Richard. You'd have to be very brave and grown-up to do that.'

Jan turned his back on her, and walked away. 'You don't know everything, Benny,' he said, sounding hurt. 'Oh no, old Benny. You don't know everything.'

'Is there something I don't know?' Miss Bennett asked him. 'Are you laughing at me, Jan?' Seizing her opportunity, she opened the door a little way. Jan stood near the french windows, whence a shaft of light from the setting sun shone across the room.

165

'Yes, yes, I'm laughing,' Jan suddenly shouted at her. 'I'm laughing because I'm so much cleverer than you are.'

He turned back into the room. Miss Bennett involuntarily gave a start and clutched the door frame. Jan took a step towards her. 'I know things you don't know,' Jan added, speaking more soberly.

'What do you know that I don't know?' Miss Bennett asked. She tried not to sound too anxious.

Jan made no reply, but merely smiled mysteriously. Miss Bennett approached him. 'Aren't you going to tell me?' she asked again, coaxingly. 'Won't you trust me with your secret?'

Jan drew away from her. 'I don't trust anybody,' he said, bitterly.

Miss Bennett changed her tone to one of puzzlement. 'I wonder, now,' she murmured. 'I wonder if perhaps you've been very clever.'

Jan giggled. 'You're beginning to see how clever I can be,' he told her.

She regarded him speculatively. 'Perhaps there are a lot of things I don't know about you,' she agreed.

'Oh, lots and lots,' Jan assured her. 'And I know a lot of things about everybody else, but I don't always tell. I get up sometimes in the night and I creep about the house. I see a lot

166

of things, and I find out a lot of things, but I don't tell.'

Adopting a conspiratorial air, Miss Bennett asked, 'Have you got some big secret now?'

Jan swung one leg over the stool, sitting astride it. 'Big secret! Big secret!' he squealed delightedly. 'You'd be frightened if you knew,' he added, laughing almost hysterically.

Miss Bennett came closer to him. 'Would I? Would I be frightened?' she asked. 'Would I be frightened of *you*, Jan?' Placing herself squarely in front of Jan, she stared intently at him.

Jan looked up at her. The expression of delight left his face, and his voice was very serious as he replied, 'Yes, you'd be very frightened of me.'

She continued to regard him closely. 'I haven't known what you were really like,' she admitted. 'I'm just beginning to understand what you're like, Jan.'

Jan's mood changes were becoming more pronounced. Sounding more and more wild, he exclaimed, 'Nobody knows anything about me really, or the things I can do.' He swung round on the stool, and sat with his back to her. 'Silly old Richard, sitting there and shooting at silly old birds.' He turned back to Miss Bennett, adding intensely, 'He didn't think anyone would shoot *him*, did he?'

'No,' she replied. 'No, that was his mistake.'

Jan rose. 'Yes, that was his mistake,' he agreed. 'He thought he could send me away, didn't he? *I* showed him.'

'Did you?' asked Miss Bennett quickly. 'How did you show him?'

Jan looked at her craftily. He paused, then finally said, 'Shan't tell you.'

'Oh, do tell me, Jan,' she pleaded.

'No,' he retorted, moving away from her. He went to the armchair and climbed into it, nestling the gun against his cheek. 'No, I shan't tell anyone.'

Miss Bennett went across to him. 'Perhaps you're right,' she told him. 'Perhaps I can guess what you did, but I won't say. It will be just your secret, won't it?'

'Yes, it's my secret,' Jan replied. He began to move restlessly about the room. 'Nobody knows what I'm like,' he exclaimed excitedly. 'I'm dangerous. They'd better be careful. Everybody had better be careful. I'm *dangerous*.'

Miss Bennett looked at him sadly. 'Richard didn't know how dangerous you were,' she said. 'He must have been surprised.'

Jan went back to the armchair, and looked into it. 'He was. He was surprised,' he agreed. 'His face went all silly. And then — and then his head dropped down when it was done,

168

and there was blood, and he didn't move any more. I showed him. I showed him! Richard won't send me away now!'

He perched on one end of the sofa, waving the gun at Miss Bennett who was trying to fight back her tears. 'Look,' Jan ordered her. 'Look. See? I've put a notch on my gun!' He tapped the gun with his knife.

'So you have!' Miss Bennett exclaimed, approaching him. 'Isn't that exciting?' She tried to grab the gun, but he was too quick for her.

'Oh, no, you don't,' he cried, as he danced away from her. 'Nobody's going to take my gun away from me. If the police come and try to arrest me, I shall shoot them.'

'There's no need to do that,' Miss Bennett assured him. 'No need at all. You're clever. You're so clever that they would never suspect you.'

'Silly old police! Silly old police!' Jan shouted jubilantly. 'And silly old Richard.' He brandished the gun at an imaginary Richard, then caught sight of the door opening. With a cry of alarm, he quickly ran off into the garden. Miss Bennett collapsed upon the sofa in tears, as Inspector Thomas hastened into the room followed by Sergeant Cadwallader.

20

'After him! Quickly!' the inspector shouted to Cadwallader as they ran into the room. The sergeant raced out onto the terrace through the french windows, as Starkwedder rushed into the room from the hallway. He was followed by Laura, who ran to the french windows and looked out. Angell was the next to appear. He, too, went across to the french windows. Mrs Warwick stood, an upright figure, in the doorway.

Inspector Thomas turned to Miss Bennett. 'There, there, dear lady,' he comforted her. 'You mustn't take on so. You did very well.'

In a broken voice, Miss Bennett replied. 'I've known all along,' she told the inspector. 'You see, I know better than anyone else what Jan is like. I knew that Richard was pushing him too far, and I knew — I've known for some time — that Jan was getting dangerous.'

'Jan!' Laura exclaimed. With a sigh of deep distress, she murmured, 'Oh, no, oh, no, not Jan.' She sank into the desk chair. 'I can't believe it,' she gasped.

Mrs Warwick glared at Miss Bennett. 'How could you, Benny?' she said, accusingly.

'How could you? I thought that at least you would be loyal.'

Miss Bennett's reply was defiant. 'There are times,' she told the old lady, 'when truth is more important than loyalty. You didn't see — any of you — that Jan was becoming dangerous. He's a dear boy — a sweet boy — but — ' Overcome with grief, she was unable to continue.

Mrs Warwick moved slowly and sadly across to the armchair and sat, staring into space.

Speaking quietly, the inspector completed Miss Bennett's thought. 'But when they get above a certain age, then they get dangerous, because they don't understand what they're doing any more,' he observed. 'They haven't got a man's judgement or control.' He went across to Mrs Warwick. 'You mustn't grieve, madam. I think I can take it upon myself to say that he'll be treated with humanity and consideration. There's a clear case to be made, I think, for his not being responsible for his actions. It'll mean detention in comfortable surroundings. And that, you know, is what it would have come to soon, in any case.' He turned away, and walked across the room, closing the hall door as he passed it.

'Yes, yes, I know you're right,' Mrs Warwick

admitted. Turning to Miss Bennett, she said, 'I'm sorry, Benny. You said that nobody else knew he was dangerous. That's not true. I knew — but I couldn't bring myself to do anything about it.'

'Somebody had to do something!' Benny replied strongly. The room fell silent, but tension mounted as they all waited for Sergeant Cadwallader's return with Jan in custody.

By the side of the road several hundred yards from the house, with a mist beginning to close in, the sergeant had got Jan cornered with a high wall behind him. Jan brandished his gun, shouting, 'Don't come any closer. No one's going to shut me away anywhere. I'll shoot you. I mean it. I'm not frightened of anyone!'

The sergeant stopped a good twenty feet away. 'Now come on, lad,' he called, coaxingly. 'No one's going to hurt you. But guns are dangerous things. Just give it to me, and come back to the house with me. You can talk to your family, and they'll help you.'

He advanced a few steps towards Jan, but stopped when the boy cried hysterically, 'I mean it. I'll shoot you. I don't care about policemen. I'm not frightened of you.'

'Of course you're not,' the sergeant replied. 'You've no reason to be frightened of me. I wouldn't hurt you. But come back into the house with me. Come on, now.' He stepped forward again, but Jan jerked the gun up and fired two shots in quick succession. The first went wide, but the second struck Cadwallader in the left hand. He gave a cry of pain, but rushed at Jan, knocking him to the ground, and attempting to get the gun away from him. As they struggled, the gun suddenly went off again. Jan gave a quick gasp, and lay silent.

Horrified, the sergeant knelt over him, staring at him in disbelief. 'No, oh no,' he murmured. 'Poor, silly boy. No! You can't be dead. Oh, please God — ' He checked Jan's pulse, then shook his head slowly. Rising to his feet, he backed slowly away for a few paces, and only then noticed that his hand was bleeding badly. Wrapping a handkerchief around it, he ran back to the house, holding his left arm in the air and gasping with pain.

By the time he got back to the french windows, he was staggering. 'Sir!' he called, as the inspector and the others ran out onto the terrace.

'What on earth's happened?' the inspector asked.

His breath coming with difficulty, the sergeant replied, 'It's terrible, what I've got to tell you.' Starkwedder helped him into the room and the sergeant staggered to the stool and sank onto it.

The inspector moved quickly to his side. 'Your hand!' he exclaimed.

'I'll see to it,' Starkwedder murmured. Holding Sergeant Cadwallader's arm, he discarded the now heavily bloodstained piece of cloth, took out a handkerchief from his own pocket, and began to tie it around the sergeant's hand.

'The mist coming on, you see,' Cadwallader began to explain. 'It was difficult to see clearly. He shot at me. Up there, along the road, near the edge of the spinney.'

With a look of horror on her face, Laura rose and went across to the french windows.

'He shot at me twice,' the sergeant was saying, 'and the second time he got me in the hand.'

Miss Bennett suddenly rose, and put her hand to her mouth. 'I tried to get the gun away from him,' the sergeant went on, 'but I was hampered with my hand, you see — '

'Yes. What happened?' the inspector prompted him.

'His finger was on the trigger,' the sergeant gasped, 'and it went off. He's shot through the heart. He's dead.'

21

Sergeant Cadwallader's announcement was greeted with a stunned silence. Laura put her hand to her mouth to stifle a cry, then slowly moved back to the desk chair and sat, staring at the floor. Mrs Warwick lowered her head and leaned on her stick. Starkwedder paced about the room, looking distracted.

'Are you sure he's dead?' the inspector asked.

'I am indeed,' the sergeant replied. 'Poor young lad, shouting defiance at me, loosing off his gun as though he loved the firing of it.'

The inspector walked across to the french windows. 'Where is he?'

'I'll come with you and show you,' the sergeant replied, struggling to his feet.

'No, you'd better stay here.'

'I'm all right now,' the sergeant insisted. 'I'll do all right until we get back to the station.' He walked out onto the terrace, swaying slightly. Looking back at the others, his face filled with misery, he murmured distractedly, ''One would not, sure, be frightful when one's dead.' That's Pope. Alexander Pope.' He shook his head, and then walked slowly away.

The inspector turned back to face Mrs Warwick and the others. 'I'm more sorry than I can say, but perhaps it's the best way out,' he said, then followed the sergeant out into the garden.

Mrs Warwick watched him go. 'The best way out!' she exclaimed, half angrily, half despairingly.

'Yes, yes,' Miss Bennett sighed. 'It is for the best. He's out of it now, poor boy.' She went to help Mrs Warwick up. 'Come, my dear, come, this has been too much for you.'

The old lady looked at her vaguely. 'I — I'll go and lie down,' she murmured, as Miss Bennett supported her to the door. Starkwedder opened it for them, and then took an envelope out of his pocket, holding it out to Mrs Warwick. 'I think you'd better have this back,' he suggested.

She turned in the doorway and took the envelope from him. 'Yes,' she replied. 'Yes, there's no need for that now.'

Mrs Warwick and Miss Bennett left the room. Starkwedder was about to close the door after them when he realized that Angell was moving across to Laura who was still sitting at the desk. She did not turn at his approach.

'May I say, madam,' Angell addressed her, 'how sorry I am. If there is anything I can do, you have only — '

Without looking up, Laura interrupted him. 'We shall need no more help from you, Angell,' she told him coldly. 'You shall have a cheque for your wages, and I should like you out of the house today.'

'Yes, madam. Thank you, madam,' Angell replied, apparently without feeling, then turned away and left the room. Starkwedder closed the door after him. The room was now growing dark, the last rays of the sun throwing shadows on the walls.

Starkwedder looked across at Laura. 'You're not going to prosecute him for blackmail?' he asked.

'No,' Laura replied, listlessly.

'A pity.' He walked over to her. 'Well, I suppose I'd better be going. I'll say goodbye.' He paused. Laura still had not looked at him. 'Don't be too upset,' he added.

'I *am* upset,' Laura responded with feeling.

'Because you loved the boy?' Starkwedder asked.

She turned to him. 'Yes. And because it's my fault. You see, Richard was right. Poor Jan should have been sent away somewhere. He should have been shut up where he couldn't do any harm. It was I who wouldn't have that. So, really, it was my fault that Richard was killed.'

'Come now, Laura, don't let's sentimental-ize,' Starkwedder retorted roughly. He came closer to her. 'Richard was killed because he asked for it. He could have shown some ordinary kindness to the boy, couldn't he? Don't you fret yourself. What you've got to do now is to be happy. Happy ever after, as the stories say.'

'Happy? With Julian?' Laura responded with bitterness in her voice. 'I wonder!' She frowned. 'You see, it isn't the same now.'

'You mean between Farrar and you?' he asked.

'Yes. You see, when I thought Julian had killed Richard, it made no difference to me. I loved him just the same.' Laura paused, then continued, 'I was even willing to say I'd done it myself.'

'I know you were,' said Starkwedder. 'More fool you. How women enjoy making martyrs of themselves!'

'But when Julian thought *I* had done it,' Laura continued passionately, 'he changed. He changed towards me completely. Oh, he was willing to try to do the decent thing and not incriminate me. But that was all.' She leaned her chin on her hand, dispirited. 'He didn't feel the same any more.'

Starkwedder shook his head. 'Look here, Laura,' he exclaimed, 'men and women don't

178

react in the same way. What it comes down to is this. Men are really the sensitive sex. Women are tough. Men can't take murder in their stride. Women apparently can. The fact is, if a man's committed a murder for a woman, it probably enhances his value in her eyes. A man feels differently.'

She looked up at him. 'You didn't feel that way,' she observed. 'When *you* thought I had shot Richard, you helped me.'

'That was different,' Starkwedder replied quickly. He sounded slightly taken aback. 'I had to help you.'

'Why did you have to help me?' Laura asked him.

Starkwedder did not reply directly. Then, after a pause, he said quietly, 'I still want to help you.'

'Don't you see,' said Laura, turning away from him, 'we're back where we started. In a way it *was* I who killed Richard because — because I was being so obstinate about Jan.'

Starkwedder drew up the stool and sat down beside her. 'That's what's eating you, really, isn't it?' he declared. 'Finding out that it was Jan who shot Richard. But it needn't be true, you know. You needn't think that unless you like.'

Laura stared at him intently. 'How can you

say such a thing?' she asked. 'I heard — we all heard — he admitted it — he boasted of it.'

'Oh, yes,' Starkwedder admitted. 'Yes, I know that. But how much do you know about the power of suggestion? Your Miss Bennett played Jan very carefully, got him all worked up. And the boy was certainly suggestible. He liked the idea, as many adolescents do, of being thought to have power, of — yes, of being a killer, if you like. Your Benny dangled the bait in front of him, and he took it. He'd shot Richard, and he put a notch on his gun, and he was a hero!' He paused. 'But you don't know — none of us really know — whether what he said was true.'

'But, for heaven's sake, he shot at the sergeant!' Laura expostulated.

'Oh, yes, he was a potential killer all right!' Starkwedder admitted. 'It's quite likely he shot Richard. But you can't say for sure that he did. It might have been — ' He hesitated. 'It might have been somebody else.'

Laura stared at him in disbelief. 'But who?' she asked, incredulously.

Starkwedder thought for a moment. Then, 'Miss Bennett, perhaps,' he suggested. 'After all, she's very fond of you all, and she might have thought it was all for the best. Or, for that matter, Mrs Warwick. Or even your boyfriend Julian — afterwards pretending that he thought you'd done it. A clever move which took you in completely.'

Laura turned away. 'You don't believe what you're saying,' she accused him. 'You're only trying to console me.'

Starkwedder looked absolutely exasperated. 'My dear girl,' he expostulated, 'anyone might have shot Richard. Even MacGregor.'

'MacGregor?' she asked, staring at him. 'But MacGregor's dead.'

'Of course he's dead,' Starkwedder replied. 'He'd have to be.' He rose and moved to the sofa. 'Look here,' he continued, 'I can put up a very pretty case for MacGregor having been the killer. Say he decided to kill Richard as revenge for the accident in which his little boy was killed.' He sat on the sofa arm. 'What does he do? Well, first thing is he has to get rid of his own personality. It wouldn't be difficult to arrange for him to be reported dead in some remote part of Alaska. It would cost a little money and some fake testimony, of course, but these things can be managed. Then he changes his name, and he starts building up a new personality for himself in some other country, some other job.'

Laura stared at him for a moment, then left the desk and went to sit in the armchair. Closing her eyes, she took a deep breath, then opened her eyes and looked at him again.

Starkwedder continued with his speculative narrative. 'He keeps tabs on what's going on over here, and when he knows that you've left Norfolk and come to this part of the world, he makes his plans. He shaves his beard, and dyes his hair, and all that sort of thing, of course. Then, on a misty night, he comes here. Now, let's say it goes like this.' He went and stood by the french windows. 'Let's say MacGregor says to Richard, 'I've got a gun, and so have you. I count three, and we both fire. I've come to get you for the death of my boy.''

Laura stared at him, appalled.

'You know,' Starkwedder went on, 'I don't think that your husband was quite the fine sporting fellow you think he was. I have an idea he mightn't have waited for a count of three. You say he was a damn good shot, but this time he missed, and the bullet went out here' — he gestured as he walked out onto the terrace — 'into the garden where there are a good many other bullets. But MacGregor doesn't miss. He shoots and kills.' Starkwedder came back into the room. 'He drops his gun by the body, takes Richard's gun, goes out of the window, and presently he comes back.'

'Comes back?' Laura asked. 'Why does he come back?'

Starkwedder looked at her for a few

182

seconds without speaking. Then, taking a deep breath, he asked, 'Can't you guess?'

Laura looked at him wonderingly. She shook her head. 'No, I've no idea,' she replied.

He continued to regard her steadily. After a pause, he spoke slowly and with an effort. 'Well,' he said, 'suppose MacGregor has an accident with his car and can't get away from here. What else can he do? Only one thing — come up to the house and discover the body!'

'You speak — ' Laura gasped, 'you speak as though you know just what happened.'

Starkwedder could no longer restrain himself. 'Of course I know,' he burst out passionately. 'Don't you understand? *I'm MacGregor!*' He leaned back against the curtains, shaking his head desperately.

Laura rose, an incredulous look on her face. She stepped towards him, half raising her arm, unable to grasp the full meaning of his words. 'You — ' she murmured. 'You — '

Starkwedder walked slowly towards Laura. 'I never meant any of this to happen,' he told her, his voice husky with emotion. 'I mean — finding you, and finding that I cared about you, and that — Oh, God, it's hopeless. Hopeless.' As she stared at him, dazed, Starkwedder took her hand and kissed the palm. 'Goodbye, Laura,' he said, gruffly.

He went quickly out through the french windows and disappeared into the mist. Laura ran out onto the terrace and called after him, 'Wait — wait. Come back!'

The mist swirled, and the Bristol fog signal began to boom. 'Come back, Michael, come back!' Laura cried. There was no reply. 'Come back, Michael,' she called again. 'Please come back! I care about you too.'

She listened intently, but heard only the sound of a car starting up and moving off. The fog signal continued to sound as she collapsed against the window and burst into a fit of uncontrollable sobbing.

THE PLAYS OF
AGATHA CHRISTIE

Alibi, the earliest Agatha Christie play to reach the stage, opening at the Prince of Wales Theatre, London, in May 1928, was not written by Christie herself. It was an adaptation by Michael Morton of her 1926 crime novel, *The Murder of Roger Ackroyd*, and Hercule Poirot was played by Charles Laughton. Christie disliked both the play and Laughton's performance. It was largely because of her dissatisfaction with *Alibi* that she decided to put Poirot on the stage in a play of her own. The result was *Black Coffee*, which ran for several months at St Martin's Theatre, London, in 1930.

Seven years passed before Agatha Christie wrote her next play, *Akhnaton*. It was not a murder mystery but the story of the ancient Pharaoh who attempted to persuade a polytheistic Egypt to turn to the worship of one deity, the sun-god Aton. *Akhnaton* failed to reach the stage in 1937, and lay forgotten for thirty-five years until, in the course of spring cleaning, its author found the typescript again and had it published.

Although she had disliked *Alibi* in 1928,

Agatha Christie gave her permission, over the years, for five more of her works to be adapted for the stage by other hands. The earliest of these was *Love From a Stranger* (1936), which Frank Vosper, a popular leading man in British theatre in the twenties and thirties, adapted from the short story 'Philomel Cottage', writing the leading male role for himself to play. The 1932 Hercule Poirot novel, *Peril at End House*, became a play of the same title in 1940, adapted by Arnold Ridley, who was well known as the author of *The Ghost Train*, a popular play of the time. With *Murder at the Vicarage*, a 1949 dramatization by Moie Charles and Barbara Toy of a 1940 novel of the same title, Agatha Christie's other popular investigator, Miss Marple, made her stage debut.

Disillusioned with one or two of these stage adaptations by other writers, in 1945 Agatha Christie had herself begun to adapt some of her already published novels for the theatre. The 1939 murder mystery *Ten Little Niggers* (a title later changed, for obvious reasons, to *And Then There Were None)* was staged very successfully both in London in 1943 and in New York the following year.

Christie's adaptation of *Appointment with Death*, a crime novel published in 1928, was staged in 1945, and two other novels which she subsequently turned into plays were *Death on the Nile* (1937), performed in 1945 as *Murder on the Nile*, and *The Hollow*, published in 1946 and staged in 1951. These three novels all featured Hercule Poirot as the investigator, but in adapting them for the stage, Christie removed Poirot. 'I had got used to having Poirot in my books,' she said of one of them, 'and so naturally he had come into this one, but he was all wrong there. He did his stuff all right, but how much better, I kept thinking, would the book have been without him. So when I came to sketch out the play, out went Poirot.'

For her next play after *The Hollow*, Agatha Christie turned not to a novel, but to her short story 'Three Blind Mice', which had itself been based on a radio play she wrote in 1947 for one of her greatest fans, Queen Mary, widow of the British monarch George V. The Queen, who was celebrating her eightieth birthday that year, had asked the BBC to commission a radio play from Agatha Christie, and 'Three Blind Mice' was the result. For its transmogrification into a stage play, a new title was found, lifted from Shakespeare's *Hamlet*. During the performance which Hamlet causes to be staged before Claudius and Gertrude, the King asks, 'What do you call the play?' to which Hamlet replies, 'The

Mousetrap'. *The Mousetrap* opened in London in November 1952, and its producer, Peter Saunders, told Christie that he had hopes for a long run of a year or even fourteen months. 'It won't run that long,' the playwright replied. 'Eight months, perhaps.' Fifty years later, *The Mousetrap* is still running, and may well go on for ever.

A few weeks into the run of *The Mousetrap*, Saunders suggested to Agatha Christie that she should adapt for the stage another of her short stories, 'Witness for the Prosecution'. But she thought this would prove too difficult, and told Saunders to try it himself. This he proceeded to do, and in due course he delivered the first draft of a play to her. When she had read it, Christie told him she did not think his version good enough, but that he had certainly shown her how it could be done. Six weeks later, she had completed the play that she later considered one of her best. On its first night in October 1953 at the Winter Garden Theatre in Drury Lane, the audience sat spellbound by the ingenuity of the surprise ending. *Witness for the Prosecution* played for 468 performances, and enjoyed an even longer run of 646 performances in New York.

Shortly after *Witness for the Prosecution* was launched, Agatha Christie agreed to write a play for the British film star, Margaret Lockwood, who wanted a role that would exploit her talent for comedy. The result was an enjoyable comedy-thriller, *Spider's Web*, which made satirical use of that creaky old device, the secret passage. In December 1954, it opened at the Savoy Theatre, where it stayed for 774 performances, joining *The Mousetrap* and *Witness for the Prosecution*. Agatha Christie had three successful plays running simultaneously in London.

For the next theatre venture, Christie collaborated with Gerald Verner to adapt *Towards Zero*, a murder mystery she had written ten years previously. Opening at St James's Theatre in September 1956, it had a respectable run of six months. The author was now in her late sixties, but still producing at least one novel a year and several short stories, as well as working on her autobiography. She was to write five more plays, all but one of them original works for the stage and not adaptations of novels. The exception was *Go Back for Murder*, a stage version of her 1943 Hercule Poirot murder mystery, *Five Little Pigs*, and once again she banished Poirot from the plot, making the investigator a personable young solicitor. The play opened at the Duchess Theatre in March 1960, but closed after only thirty-one performances.

Her four remaining plays, all original stage works, were *Verdict, The Unexpected Guest* (both first staged in 1958), *Rule of Three* (1962), and *Fiddlers Three* (1972). *Rule of Three* is actually three unconnected one-act plays, the last of which, 'The Patient', is an excellent mystery thriller with an unbeatable final line. However, audiences stayed away from this evening of three separate plays, and *Rule of Three* closed at the Duchess Theatre after ten weeks.

Christie's final work for the theatre, *Fiddlers Three*, did not even reach London. It toured the English provinces in 1971 as *Fiddlers Five*, was withdrawn to be rewritten, and reopened at the Yvonne Arnaud Theatre, Guildford, in August 1972. After touring quite successfully for several weeks, it failed to find a suitable London theatre and closed out-of-town.

Verdict, which opened at London's Strand Theatre in May 1958, is unusual in that, although a murder does occur in the play, there is no mystery attached to it, for it is committed in full view of the audience. It closed after a month, but its resilient author murmured, 'At least I am glad *The Times* liked it,' immediately set to work to write another play, and completed it within four weeks. This was *The Unexpected Guest*, which, after a week in Bristol, moved to the Duchess Theatre, London, where it opened in August 1958 and had a satisfactory run of eighteen months. One of the best of Agatha Christie's plays, its dialogue is taut and effective, and its plot full of surprises, despite being economical and not over-complex. Reviews were uniformly enthusiastic, and now, more than forty years later, it has begun a new lease of life as a novel.

A few months before her death in 1976, Agatha Christie gave her consent for a stage adaptation to be made by Leslie Darbon of her 1950 novel, *A Murder is Announced*, which featured Miss Marple. When the play reached the stage posthumously in 1977, the critic of *The Financial Times* predicted that it would run as long as *The Mousetrap*. It did not.

In 1981, Leslie Darbon adapted one more Christie novel, *Cards on the Table*, a Poirot murder mystery published forty-five years earlier. Taking a leaf from the author's book where Hercule Poirot was concerned, Darbon removed him from the cast of characters. To date, there have been no more stage adaptations of Agatha Christie novels. With *Black Coffee*, *The Unexpected Guest*, and now *Spider's Web*, I have started a trend in the opposite direction.

CHARLES OSBORNE

We do hope that you have enjoyed reading this large print book.

Did you know that all of our titles are available for purchase?

We publish a wide range of high quality large print books including:
Romances, Mysteries, Classics
General Fiction
Non Fiction and Westerns

Special interest titles available in large print are:
The Little Oxford Dictionary
Music Book
Song Book
Hymn Book
Service Book

Also available from us courtesy of Oxford University Press:
Young Readers' Dictionary
(large print edition)
Young Readers' Thesaurus
(large print edition)

For further information or a free brochure, please contact us at:
Ulverscroft Large Print Books Ltd.,
The Green, Bradgate Road, Anstey,
Leicester, LE7 7FU, England.
Tel: (00 44) 0116 236 4325
Fax: (00 44) 0116 234 0205

Other titles published by Ulverscroft:

BLACK COFFEE

Agatha Christie and Charles Osborne

Fearing for the security of his revolutionary new formula for a powerful explosive, Sir Claud Amory requests the assistance of Hercule Poirot in transferring it safely to the Ministry of Defence. But when the formula disappears from its safe, Amory must change his plans. Locking his houseguests in the library, he informs them that the thief has precisely one minute of darkness in which to return the formula anonymously — or face the great detective even now on his way. The lights go off; by the time they come on again, Amory is dead in his arm-chair . . .

DESTINATION UNKNOWN

Agatha Christie

When a number of leading scientists disappear without trace, concern grows within the international intelligence community — and the one woman who appears to hold the key to the mystery is dying from injuries sustained in a plane crash. Meanwhile, in a Casablanca hotel room, Hilary Craven prepares to take her own life. But her suicide attempt is about to be interrupted by a man who will offer her an altogether more thrilling way to die . . .

THEY CAME TO BAGHDAD

Agatha Christie

Baghdad is holding a secret superpower summit, but the word is out, and an underground organisation in the Middle East is plotting to sabotage the talks. Into this explosive situation appears Victoria Jones, a girl with a yearning for adventure who gets more than she bargains for when a wounded spy dies in her hotel room. The only man who can save the summit is dead. Can Victoria make sense of his dying words: '. . . Lucifer . . . Basrah . . . Lefarge . . .'?

CROOKED HOUSE

Agatha Christie

The Leonideses are one big happy family living in a sprawling, ramshackle mansion. That is until the head of the household, Aristide, is murdered with a fatal injection. Suspicion naturally falls on the old man's young widow, fifty years his junior. But the murderer has reckoned without the tenacity of Charles Hayward, fiance of the late millionaire's granddaughter . . .